L
and other stories

THE ANNIVERSARY EDITION OF HERMAN CHARLES BOSMAN

Planning began in late 1997 — the fiftieth anniversary of Bosman's first collection in book form, Mafeking Road *— to re-edit his works in their original, unabridged and uncensored texts. The project should be completed by 2005 — the centenary of his birth.*

GENERAL EDITORS:
STEPHEN GRAY AND CRAIG MACKENZIE

Already published in this edition:
MAFEKING ROAD AND OTHER STORIES
WILLEMSDORP
COLD STONE JUG
IDLE TALK: VOORKAMER STORIES (I)
JACARANDA IN THE NIGHT
OLD TRANSVAAL STORIES
VERBORGE SKATTE
SEED-TIME AND HARVEST AND OTHER STORIES
A CASK OF JEREPIGO

Herman Charles Bosman

UNTO DUST
and other stories

The Anniversary Edition

Edited by Craig MacKenzie

HUMAN & ROUSSEAU
Cape Town Pretoria Johannesburg

Copyright © 2002 by The estate of Herman Charles Bosman
Original edition first published by Human & Rousseau in 1963
This selection and introduction © Craig MacKenzie, 2002
Revised Anniversary edition published in 2002 by Human & Rousseau
28 Wale Street, Cape Town

Cover photo from H. F. Gros's album, *A Pictorial Description of the Transvaal*, taken at Moord Drift on the Nylstroom, Waterberg District, in 1888.
Back cover portrait of Herman Charles Bosman, taken in Johannesburg by an unknown photographer and first used in *The South African Jewish Times* in October, 1948.
Design and typeset in 11 on 13 pt Times by Alinea Studio, Cape Town
Printed and bound by Mills Litho,
Maitland, Cape Town, South Africa

ISBN 0 7981 4277 4

No part of this book may be reproduced or transmitted in any form or by any means, electronic or mechanical or by photocopying, recording or microfilming, or stored in any retrieval system, without the written permission of the publisher

Herman Charles Bosman (1905–1951) was born in Kuils River near Cape Town but lived in the Transvaal for most of his life. Educated at the University of the Witwatersrand, he was sent as a novice teacher to the Marico District in what was then the Western Transvaal. There he encountered spellbinding storytellers whom he was later to immortalise in his fictional invention Oom Schalk Lourens, teller of all of the stories gathered here.

Bosman was convicted of the murder of his step-brother in 1926 and spent four years in Pretoria Central prison. Upon his release he embarked on a career as a journalist and began writing short stories. Among these were his famous Oom Schalk stories, gathered in *Mafeking Road* (1947; re-edited for the Anniversary Edition in 1998) and in *Seed-time and Harvest and Other Stories* (2001), and concluded in the present volume.

Unto Dust originally appeared posthumously under the editorship of Lionel Abrahams in 1963. This new *Unto Dust* is completely re-edited and includes previously unpublished and uncollected stories.

Contents

Introduction 9

Romaunt of the Smuggler's Daughter 25
The Picture of Gysbert Jonker 33
Treasure Trove 39
The Ferreira Millions 44
Unto Dust 49
Bush Telegraph 53
The Homecoming 58
Susannah and the Play-actor 62
Sold Down the River 66
Tryst by the Vaal 71
The Lover Who Came Back 75
The Selon's Rose 80
When the Heart is Eager 86
The Brothers 91
Oom Piet's Party 97
The Missionary 103
Funeral Earth 108
The Red Coat 113
The Question 119
Peaches Ripening in the Sun 124
The Traitor's Wife 129

Notes on the Text 134

Introduction

Bosman wrote sixty-one stories in his famous Oom Schalk Lourens sequence; they have never before been available to the reader in an orderly and correct fashion.

Twenty of these stories he selected for *Mafeking Road* (first published in 1947 and re-edited as *Mafeking Road and Other Stories* for the Anniversary Edition in 1998). For the Anniversary Edition the remaining forty-one Oom Schalks have been arranged in order of publication and divided into two groups. The first twenty have appeared in *Seed-time and Harvest and Other Stories* (2001) and the present volume, *Unto Dust and Other Stories*, gathers the remaining twenty-one Oom Schalks. The latter stories were published in an intense period between September, 1948, and February, 1951, and are the last Oom Schalk stories that Bosman wrote.

The title of this volume will be known to readers of Bosman. Following Barney Simon's suggestion, Lionel Abrahams chose it when he put together his original edition of *Unto Dust* (1963). The sustained success of *Mafeking Road*, and the fact that Bosman had left dozens of stories uncollected at his death, encouraged Abrahams to do what Bosman had intended, but was never able to undertake – i.e. to put together a further collection of bushveld stories.

Abrahams's first attempt at gathering Bosman's uncollected pieces had resulted in the collection of essays and sketches, *A Cask of Jerepigo* (1957; re-edited with new contents for the Anniversary Edition and published alongside the present volume). He turned next to the uncollected short stories, using as his sources the periodicals in which the stories were first published and also the cache of typescripts Helena Lake (Bosman's widow, now remarried) had left in his charge. (Helena had granted him permission to gather the scattered writings and attempt to get them published in various forms.)

In an unpublished memoir (March, 2002) on the process of getting *Unto Dust* into print, Abrahams makes the following points:

> The stories excluded from *Unto Dust* as eventually published fall into four groups. The first was perhaps not as many as three stories I judged to be versions of others I was including and

liked better; the second was stories I felt did not worthily represent Bosman's art. . . ; the third group was the few stories I was obliged to excise from my collection when Anthony Blond decided that economic considerations required it to be reduced in quantity; the fourth was stories my research failed to discover.

As regards the running order, he notes: "Whim, essentially, dictated the order in which I arranged the stories. There needed to be a strong opening story ['Unto Dust'] and an aesthetically appropriate final one ['Funeral Earth']. Notions of thematic grouping and contrast may have governed the general sequence."

The process of finding a publisher for *Unto Dust* proved to be a difficult one. The initial commercial failure of *A Cask of Jerepigo* dissuaded Abrahams from approaching the CNA, the original publishers of that volume. Instead, he tried the London firm Jonathan Cape, for whom the former South African, William Plomer, worked. Abrahams had heard an address given by Plomer on the latter's visit to Johannesburg in 1956 in which he had expressed an enthusiasm for South African literature, and for Bosman in particular: "*Mafeking Road* seems to me a real work of art. . . Bosman's irony is delightful, and not merely on the surface. In story after story he brings into focus an ironical situation of a kind that throws into relief the common humanity of his characters" (*Proceedings of a Conference of Writers, Publishers, Editors and University Teachers of English*, 1956).

Abrahams's hopes that Plomer's enthusiasm would be enough to persuade Cape were dashed, however: "I recall collecting the returned typescript from the Kensington post office, then sitting on a bench in Rhodes Park nursing the parcel with a huge sense of defeat." None the less, through the agency of a friend who was working for the firm at the time, Abrahams did eventually manage to secure a British publisher for *Unto Dust*, and the volume duly appeared in a joint British–South African edition (Anthony Blond, London, and Human and Rousseau, Cape Town). Besides Blond's cutbacks, the first printing of *Unto Dust* ended in a howler – the classic last paragraphs of "Funeral Earth" had gone missing. The Blond connection did not extend beyond this one title, either, but it was the beginning of an extremely successful relationship between Human and Rousseau and Bosman (through Abrahams and Helena Lake).

The British edition of *Unto Dust* did not sell well, so that when Blond remaindered its edition the unsold stock was taken over by Human and Rousseau. The more successful Human and Rousseau *Unto Dust* was

Cover of the periodical Fighting Talk, *August, 1958. The Bosman story featured was "Funeral Earth."*

quickly followed by their edition of *A Cask of Jerepigo* (1964) and of Abrahams's enormously popular sampler *Bosman at His Best* (1965). In 1969 *Cold Stone Jug* and *Mafeking Road* were taken up in the Human and Rousseau 'uniform edition' of Bosman's works; the series was now firmly established and steadily supplemented by other titles.

Abrahams's approach to Plomer did result in the latter writing a very perceptive foreword to *Unto Dust* in which he celebrated Bosman's "playful irony", and "sly, mocking, humorous Afrikaner intelligence." In the stories, Plomer went on, we see how this intelligence "punctures pretentiousness and notices the little humbugs and evasions and peculations that go on among ordinary, sober, respectable citizens." Bosman's achievement, he concluded, was to have "presented local and

*The Abe Berry illustration that accompanied the first publication of "Unto Dust" in English (*Trek*, Feb., 1949)*

remote involvements of passion, love, hate, fidelity, infidelity, history and death in such a way that they are made universally human, and to have maintained while doing so his light and entertaining touch. What an uncommon gift!"

Plomer's foreword set the tone for the reviews that followed. *News/Check* (29 March, 1963), for example, carried a lengthy article providing some background to Bosman and his stories and comparing him favourably to Pauline Smith, whose "poetry" he was said to share. Some stories were adjudged "simple to the point of banality", but all were redeemed by "the deceptively casual skill of manipulation: story after story leaps into poignant new significance in its very last sentence."

Mary Morison Webster, friend and admirer of Bosman (but someone who could also be coolly even-handed when the occasion required), claimed that the writer had "a unique gift" and his storytelling "a delightful spontaneity" (*Sunday Times*, 14 April, 1963): "Words, sentences and images flow from his pen, bubble forth from the confines of his imagination, with the naturalness and exuberance of a mountain spring." Webster was too astute to be fooled by surface appearances, however: "The seeming artlessness of his style is nevertheless deceptive. On numerous occasions, he gives an inkling of the subtleties of his technique when, at intervals in a story, he repeats the phrase or string of words which is its motif." She adds: "Through the eyes of Oom Schalk, Bosman looks on impartially at the goings-on described. He exposes hypocrisy and cant, pokes amiable fun at 'Rooineks' where they occur, and, in general, surveys the human scene in Marico with his tongue in his cheek." The story "Unto Dust" is singled out in particular as an example of Bosman's "oblique" way of exposing the "stupidity and unreason" of the racist attitudes of the Marico farmers.

By the 1960s Afrikaans-language critics, who had previously ignored Bosman, were also beginning to share in the new enthusiasm. A long review in *Die Huisgenoot* (26 July, 1963), for example, welcomed the new collection with the fulsome praise that "Wie ook al vantevore kennis gemaak het met die werk van Herman Charles Bosman – veral *Mafeking Road* – sal in hierdie posthume bundel 'n waardige en merkwaardige toevoeging tot die Suid-Afrikaanse kortverhaalskat vind." "Unto Dust" and "The Selon's Rose" are singled out for special praise, and although Bosman is criticised for the supposedly sometimes excessive use of Afrikaans words where they are not really functional, and also for some unnecessary digressions and circumlocutions, the reviewer concludes: "'n Kortverhaalbundel soos dié, met sy rypheid, oorwoënheid, tegniese meesterskap, en menslike deernis wat woord geword het, word daar nie dikwels gepubliseer nie."

The doyen A. P. Grové in *Die Vaderland* (May, 1963) called the collection "'n pragtige bydrae tot die Suid-Afrikaanse Engelse prosa", and went on to say that "die beste van hierdie verhale gunstig vergelyk met dié van Plomer self asook dié van Pauline Smith." Arguing that Bosman knew his region and its characters more intimately than these

Oom Schalk's Zeerust in the Western Transvaal, shortly after the Second Anglo-Boer War. (Courtesy of the National Archives, Pretoria.)

The Marico Commando circa 1910

The landmark Lutheran church over the border at Ramoutsa (Photo by S. Gray)

The illustration that accompanied the first publication of "The Traitor's Wife" (Spotlight, Feb., 1951; artist: 'Flip')

two better-known contemporaries, and that examples of "lewendigheid en geestigheid" are to be found on every page, he goes on to make special mention of "Peaches Ripening in the Sun" and "The Picture of Gysbert Jonker." Bosman's insight that the dreams that people have frequently founder on the hard rocks of reality, he concludes, gives these "'lokale' verhale 'n universele betekenis."

The first longer assessment of *Unto Dust* came from Lewis Nkosi in exile in Paris in *South Africa: Information and Analysis* (September, 1969). Nkosi begins by noting that Bosman "the celebrated humorist" may have been overlooked abroad because of the "committed *South Africanness*" of his subject matter. None the less, Bosman's humour, he observes, "is of the simplest type and depends largely on the careful demolition of false grandeur, pride and social pretences of his rural Boers, whose defeat occurs toward the end of each story rather like the skilfully engineered fall of the small-town bully in a Western or some similar type of story." Notwithstanding his considerable skills, however, according to Nkosi, Bosman "in the end lamentably fails to evoke a country larger than a locality."

But almost in spite of himself, even Nkosi ends with some admiring comments. Styling Bosman a "twentieth-century buccaneer" and re-

The Paul de Groot theatre company touring in 1926, with Mathilde Hanekom and Paul de Groot in front, André Huguenet in the third window and Wena Naudé, extreme right. A scene reminiscent of "Sold Down the River." (Courtesy of the National Film Archives, Pretoria.)

viewing in some detail his narrative technique, he concludes that the writer's great achievement was not to have "merge[d] his identity completely with that of his urban compatriots, English and Afrikaner... He went in search of the 'true' Afrikaners. What he found may leave a black reader with a sour taste in the mouth but my God it *was* a find!"

So, in sum, by the time of *Unto Dust* Bosman's standing had become firmly established.

There are significant differences between Abraham's *Unto Dust* and the present volume. Nine of the twenty-one stories printed here do not appear in Abrahams's collection and two that occur in both books – "The Lover Who Came Back" and "The Brothers" – do so in significantly different versions (see Notes on the Text for details). Of the nine stories that

The illustration that accompanied the first publication of "The Missionary"
(Spotlight, *Jan., 1951; artist unknown)*

do not appear in Abrahams's *Unto Dust*, two are previously unpublished ("Bush Telegraph" and "Tryst by the Vaal") and two have appeared in print only once before now and have never been taken up in any collections of Bosman's stories ("Susannah and the Play-actor" and "Oom Piet's Party"). The remaining five were not selected by Abrahams, but have appeared in other posthumous Bosman collections. On the other hand, thanks to the larger scope available to an editor nowadays in the Anniversary Edition, several stories which Abrahams selected but which did not involve Oom Schalk as a narrator have been collected with others of their type in *Old Transvaal Stories* (2000).

The two previously unpublished stories were found in typescript in the archives of the Harry Ransom Humanities Research Center (HRHRC) at the University of Texas at Austin. "Bush Telegraph" is a variation of a story Bosman published in Afrikaans ("Die Kaffertamboer"), but no complete English version has survived. I have reverted to the earlier (and significantly different) "Bush Telegraph" here, as it is wholly Bosman's own work and has the additional interest of never having appeared in print before.

Two typescripts relating to "Tryst by the Vaal" are held by the HRHRC. The first of these is untitled and incomplete; this version Bosman translated into Afrikaans and published as "Ontmoetingplek aan die Vaal" in May, 1949. "Tryst by the Vaal" is a later, shorter and far more effective version, but has until now lain unnoticed among the other Bosman papers at the HRHRC. A detailed examination of these typescripts reveals an interesting pattern in Bosman's writing technique. He frequently drafted a long, over-explanatory version of a story, and then returned later to cut it (sometimes quite drastically) in order to allow a leaner, more evocative narrative to emerge.

It has been a common critical fallacy down the years to suppose that Bosman's Oom Schalk stories are merely simple, unsophisticated tales that flowed with prolific ease from the writer's pen. On the occasion of the appearance of this, the last volume in the three-part Oom Schalk series in the Anniversary Edition, it is appropriate finally to lay this misconception to rest. The scores of Bosman manuscripts held by the HRHRC reveal that Bosman was in fact an assiduous, painstaking writer who worked extremely hard at making his prose style seem effortless.

He typically began by drafting a story in pencil on half-leaves of jotting paper (the 'half-scaps' favoured by journalists). This draft he revised extensively before typing it up, again on half-leaves. (He did this in order both to reduce the amount of retyping necessary should a major change be required and also to be able to lay out the various movements of the story in jigsaw-puzzle fashion.) Changes to this draft were again added by hand, and it would be followed by a near-final typed version on full pages. Often this penultimate draft was again corrected and fine-tuned before a final version was sent off to a magazine for publication.

In all, then, three or even four separate drafts were written or typed, and most of these contained holograph emendations, which means that many stories were thoroughly reviewed and revised at least six times. Of course, given Bosman's disorderly life, this process was not followed in all instances; but it does represent his preferred method of going to work as a writer, particularly in the mature and final phase represented by the stories in the present volume. "The Traitor's Wife", the powerful finale to this collection, provides a good example of his modus operandi (see Notes on the Text for a detailed discussion).

Bosman's sophistication and devotion to his craft is also evident in his ironic intertextual play. Keats's "[a]lone and palely loitering" knight ("La Belle Dame sans Merci", 1819) becomes "that fellow by the dam, looking all pale and upset about something" in the mouth of the robust Fritz Pretorius, whose aesthetic range does not extend to the Romantics ("Romaunt of the Smuggler's Daughter"). "The Picture of Gysbert Jonker" is a cunning backveld play on Oscar Wilde's gothic, fin-de-siècle *The Picture of Dorian Gray* (1890). And in "Sold Down the River" Bosman brings Harriet Beecher Stowe's *Uncle Tom's Cabin* (1852) into Zeerust and reflects ironically on the way the villain becomes the hero and vice versa when the script is revised in accordance with bushveld tastes.

Nor did Bosman steer away from controversy when his conscience was pricked. The centrepiece of this collection, "Unto Dust", is a swingeing attack on the growing policy in postwar Nationalist South African politics to discriminate on grounds of race. As Plomer ironically noted in his foreword quoted earlier, "in 'Unto Dust' the anatomy of a black proves, in certain circumstances, regrettably indistinguishable from that of a white." (Regrettable, that is, to white bigots.) And in "The Missionary", a much bolder version of his earlier story "Graven Image", a black wood-carver's unerring gift for creating a likeness (flattering or otherwise) deflates the pomposity of the missionary, whose condescension towards his black charges is shown to be entirely misplaced.

So we laugh, with the author, at his characters' occasional narrow-mindedness and even cussed stupidity. Oom Schalk's simplicity is therefore only apparent, and the intelligence guiding this figure was possessed by a worldly-wise, erudite man who knew that the best way of kindling people's imaginations and touching their emotions was by using plain, everyday language and dealing with events that, while they lay within their experiential ambit, had far wider applications.

In April, 1954, the poet Roy Campbell broadcast his "Some South African Writers" over the SABC. There he described Bosman's Oom Schalk stories as "full of poetry, humour, pathos, tragedy and comedy, all mingled inseparably without dislocating the unity of his style which is so consummately contrived as to be unnoticeable." He went on to remark that Bosman's satire "is all the more powerful for being kindly and restrained"; that his work "appeals to all classes of readers, highbrow or lowbrow, simultaneously at once"; and that his name "will one day be a household word in South Africa."

With him, South Africans have since come to agree; all of Campbell's comments have proved to be trenchant, and the last of them particularly so. Bosman's name *has* become a household word, and this is due in large measure to the enduring success of his Oom Schalk stories, particularly thanks to Lionel Abrahams for having launched them under this title with such flare.

The present collection completes the three-part Oom Schalk sequence of the Anniversary Edition, bringing to a close the entire series of tales told by South Africa's most famous yarn-spinner. His mouth may thus be stopped, but there is no doubt that his stories will continue to resonate for readers in the years to come.

Craig MacKenzie
Johannesburg, 2002

Patrick Mynhardt at the Market Theatre, Johannesburg, in one of his famous Oom Schalk Lourens performances. (Photo: Ruphin Coudyzer.)

Romaunt of the Smuggler's Daughter

Long ago, there was more money (Oom Schalk Lourens said, wistfully) to be made out of cattle-smuggling that there is in these times. The Government knows that, of course. But the Government thinks that why we Marico farmers don't bring such large herds of native cattle across the Bechuanaland border anymore, on moonless nights, is because the mounted police are more efficient than they used to be.

That isn't the reason, of course.

You still get as good a sort of night as ever – a night when there is only the light of the stars shining on the barbed wire that separates the Transvaal from the Protectorate. But why my wire-cutters are rusting in the buitekamer from disuse is not because the border is better patrolled than it was in the old days. For it is not the mounted police, with their polished boots and clicking spurs, but the barefoot Bechuana kaffirs that have grown more cunning.

We all said that it was the fault of the mission school at Ramoutsa, of course. Afterwards, when more schools were opened, deeper into the Protectorate, we gave those schools a share of the blame as well... Naturally, it wasn't a thing that happened suddenly. Only, we found, as the years went by, that the kaffirs in the Bechuanaland Protectorate wanted more and more for their cattle. And later on they would traffic with us only when we paid them in hard cash; they frowned on the idea of barter.

I can still remember the look of grieved wonderment on Jurie Prinsloo's face when he told us about his encounter with the Bapedi chief near Malopolole. Jurie came across the Bapedi chief in front of his hut. And the Bapedi chief was not squatting on an animal skin spread on the ground; instead, he was sitting on a real chair, and looking quite comfortable sitting in it, too.

"Here's a nice, useful roll of copper wire for you," Jurie Prinsloo said to the Bapedi chief, who was lazily scratching the back of his instep against the lower cross-piece of the chair. "You can give me an ox for it. That red ox, there, with the long horns and the loose dewlap will be all right. They don't know any better about an ox on the Johannesburg market."

"But what can I do with the copper wire?" the Bapedi chief asked. "I have not got a telephone."

This was a real problem for Jurie Prinsloo, of course. For many years he had been trading rolls of copper wire for kaffir cattle, and it had never occurred to him to think out what the kaffirs used the wire for.

"Well," Jurie Prinsloo said, weakly, "you can make it into a ring to put through your nose, and you can also – "

But even as Jurie Prinsloo spoke, he realised that the old times had passed away for ever.

And we all said, yes, it was these missionaries, with the schools they were opening up all over the place, who were ruining the kaffirs. As if the kaffirs weren't uncivilised enough in the first place, we said. And now the missionaries had to come along and educate them on top of it.

Anyway, the superior sort of smile that came across the left side of the chief's face, at the suggestion that he should wear a copper ring in his nose, made Jurie Prinsloo feel that he had to educate the Bapedi chief some more. What was left of the chair, after Jurie Prinsloo had finished educating the Bapedi chief, was produced in the magistrate's court in Gaborone, where Jurie Prinsloo was fined ten pounds for assault with intent to do grievous bodily harm. In those days you could buy quite a few head of cattle for ten pounds.

And, in spite of his schooling, the Bapedi chief remained as ignorant as ever. For, during the rest of the time that he remained head of the tribe, he would not allow a white man to enter his stat again.

But, as I have said, it was different, long ago. Then the Bechuanaland kaffirs would still take an interest in their appearance, and they would be glad to exchange their cattle for brass and beads and old whale-bone corsets and tins of axle-grease (to make the skin on their chests shine) and cheap watches. They would even come and help us drive the cattle across the line, just for the excitement of it, and to show off their new finery, in the way of umbrellas and top-hats and pieces of pink underwear, at the kraals through which we passed.

Easily the most enterprising cattle-smuggler in the Marico Bushveld at the time of which I am talking was Gerrit Oosthuizen. He had a farm right next to the Protectorate border. So that the barbed wire that he cut at night, when he brought over a herd of cattle, was also the fence of his own farm. Within a few years Gerrit Oosthuizen had made so much money out of smuggled cattle that he was able to introduce a large number of improvements on his farm, including a new type of concrete cattle dip with iron steps, and a piano for which he had a special kind of stand built into the floor of his voorkamer, so as to keep the white ants away.

Gerrit Oosthuizen's daughter, Jemima, who was then sixteen years of age and very pretty, with dark hair and a red mouth and a soft shadow at the side of her throat, started learning to play the piano. Farmers and their wives from many miles away came to visit Gerrit Oosthuizen. They came to look at the piano stand, which had been specially designed by a Pretoria engineer, and had an aluminium tank underneath that you kept filled with water, so that it was impossible for the white ants to effect much damage – if you wiped them off from the underneath part of the piano with a paraffin rag every morning.

The visitors would come to the farm, and they would drink coffee in the voorkamer, and they would listen to Jemima Oosthuizen playing a long piece out of a music book with one finger, and they would nod their heads solemnly, at the end of it, when Jemima sat very still, with her dark hair falling forward over her eyes, and they would say, well, if that Pretoria engineer thought that, in the long run, the white ants would not be able to find a way of beating his aluminium invention, and of eating up all the inside of the piano, then they didn't know the Marico white ant, that's all.

We who were visitors to the Oosthuizen farm spoke almost with pride of the cleverness of the white ant. We felt, somehow, that the white ants belonged to the Marico Bushveld, just like we did, and we didn't like the idea of a Pretoria engineer, who was an uitlander, almost, thinking that with his invention – which consisted just of bits of shiny tin – he would be able to outwit the cunning of a Marico white ant.

Through his conducting his cattle-smuggling operations on so large and successful a scale, Gerrit Oosthuizen soon got rich. He was respected – and even envied – throughout the Marico. They say that when the Volksraad member came to Gerrit Oosthuizen's farm, and he saw around him so many unmistakable signs of great wealth, including green window-blinds that rolled up by themselves when you jerked the sashcord – they say that even the Volksraad member was very much impressed, and that he seemed to be deep in thought for a long time. It almost seemed as though he was wondering whether, in having taken up politics, he had chosen the right career, after all.

If that was how the Volksraad member really did feel about the matter, then it must have been a sad thing for him, when the debates in the Raadsaal at Pretoria dragged far into the night, and he had to remain seated on his back bench, without having much heart in the proceedings, since he would be dreaming all the time of a herd of red cattle being driven towards a fence in the starlight. And when the Chairman of the Committee called another member to order, it might almost have sounded to this Volksraad member as though it was a voice coming out of the shadows of the maroelas and demanding, suddenly, "Who goes there?"

To this question – which he had heard more than once, of course, during the years in which he had smuggled cattle – Gerrit Oosthuizen nearly always had the right answer. It was always more difficult for Gerrit Oosthuizen if it was a youthful-sounding voice shouting out that challenge. Because it usually meant, then, that the uniformed man on horseback, half hidden in the shadow of a withaak, was a young recruit, anxious to get promotion. Gerrit Oosthuizen could not handle him in the same way as he could an elderly mounted police sergeant, who was a married man with a number of children, and who had learnt, through long years of service, a deeper kind of wisdom about life on this old earth.

It was, each time, through mistaken zeal on the part of a young recruit – who nearly always got a transfer, shortly afterwards – that Gerrit Oosthuizen had to stand his trial in the Zeerust courthouse. He was several times acquitted. On a few occasions he was fined quite heavily. Once he was sentenced to six months' imprisonment without the option of a fine. Consequently, while Gerrit Oosthuizen was known to entertain a warm regard for almost any middle-aged mounted policeman with a fat stomach, he invariably displayed a certain measure of impatience towards a raw recruit. It was said that on more than one occasion, in the past, Gerrit Oosthuizen had given expression to his impatience by discharging a couple of Mauser bullets – aimed high – into the shadows from which an adolescent voice had spoken out of turn.

Needless to say, all these stories that went the rounds of the Marico about Gerrit Oosthuizen only added to his popularity with the farmers. Even when the predikant shook his head, on being informed of Gerrit Oosthuizen's latest escapade, you could see that he regarded it as being but little more than a rather risky sort of prank, and that, if anything, he admired Gerrit Oosthuizen, the Marico's champion cattle-smuggler, for the careless way in which he defied the law. Whatever he did, Gerrit Oosthuizen always seemed to act in the right way. And it seems to me that, if he adheres to such a kind of rule, the man who goes against the law gets as much respect from the people around him as does the law-giver. More, even.

"The law stops on the south side of the Dwarsberge," Gerrit Oosthuizen said to a couple of his neighbours, in a sudden burst of pride, on the day that the piano arrived and was placed on top of the patent aluminium stand. "And north of the Dwarsberge I am the law."

But soon after that Gerrit Oosthuizen did something that the Marico farmers did not understand, and that they did not forgive him for so easily. Just at the time when his daughter, Jemima, was most attractive, and was beginning to play herself in on the piano, using two fingers of each hand – and when quite a number of the young men of the district were beginning to pay court to her – Gerrit Oosthuizen sent her away to the seminary for young ladies that had just been opened in Zeerust.

We expressed our surprise to Gerrit Oosthuizen in various ways. After all, we all liked Jemima, and it didn't seem right that an attractive Bushveld girl should be sent away like that to get spoilt. She would come back with city affectations and foreign ways. She would no longer be able to make a good, simple wife for an honest Boer lad. It was, of course, the young men who expressed this view with the greatest measure of indignation – even those who were not so particularly honest, either, perhaps.

But Gerrit Oosthuizen said, no, he believed in his daughter having the best opportunities. There were all sorts of arts and graces of life that she would learn at the finishing-school, he said. Among the Marico's young men, however, were some who thought that there was very little that any young ladies' seminary would be able to teach Jemima that she did not already know.

We lost confidence in Gerrit Oosthuizen after that, of course. And when next we got up a deputation to the Government to protest about the money being spent on native education – because there were already signs of a falling-off in the cattle trade with the Bechuanas – then we did not elect Gerrit Oosthuizen as a delegate. We felt that his ideas on education, generally, were becoming unsound.

It is true, however, that, during the time that Jemima was at the seminary, Gerrit Oosthuizen did once or twice express doubts about his wisdom in having sent her there.

"Jemima writes to say that she is reading a lot of poetry," Gerrit Oosthuizen said to me, once. "I wonder if that isn't perhaps, sort of. . . you know. . ."

I agreed with Gerrit that it seemed as if his daughter was embarking on something dangerous. But she was still very young, I added. She might yet grow out of that sort of foolishness. I said that when the right young man for her came along she would close that book of poetry quick enough, without even bothering to mark the place that she had got up to. Nevertheless, I was glad to think that Gerrit Oosthuizen was not so happy, anymore, about his daughter's higher education.

"Still, she gets very good reports from her teachers," Gerrit Oosthuizen said, but without any real enthusiasm. "Especially from her poetry teacher."

Meanwhile, the cattle-smuggling business was going from bad to worse, and by the time Jemima returned from her stay at the seminary, Gerrit Oosthuizen had his hands full with his personal affairs. He had made a few singularly unsuccessful cattle-smuggling trips into the Protectorate. By that time the kaffirs had got so educated that one squint-eyed Mtosa even tried to fall back on barter – but the other way around. He wanted Gerrit Oosthuizen to trade his mules and cart for a piece of glass that the Mtosa claimed was a Namaqualand diamond. And, on top of everything else, when Gerrit Oosthuizen did on a few occasions get back into the Transvaal with a likely herd of cattle, it was with Daniel Malan, a new recruit to the border patrol, hot on his trail.

It was under these circumstances that Jemima Oosthuizen returned to the Bushveld farm from the young ladies' seminary in Zeerust. Just to look at her, it seemed that the time she had spent at the finishing-school had not changed her very much. If anything, she was even prettier than she had been before she left. Her lips were still curved and red. There was still that soft shadow at the side of her throat. Only, it seemed to me that in her dark eyes there was now a dreamy look that wouldn't fit in too readily with the everyday life of a Bushveld farm.

And I was right. And it didn't take the young fellows of the neighbourhood very long to find out, either, that Jemima Oosthuizen had, indeed, changed. It saddened them to realise that they could do very little about it.

Jemima Oosthuizen was, as always, friendly to each young man who called. But it was easy for these young men to detect that it was a general sort of friendliness – which she felt for them all equally and alike. She would read poetry to them, reading and explaining to them passages out of the many books of verse that she had brought back with her. And while they were very ready to be thrilled – even when they knew that it was a foolish waste of time – yet they felt that there was no way in which they could make any progress with her. No matter what any young man might feel about her, Jemima's feelings for him remained impersonal.

"What's wrong with me?" Andries Steyn asked of a number of young men, once. "She can go on reading that poetry to me as long as she likes.

I don't mind. I don't understand anything about it, in any case. But the moment I start holding her hand, I know that she isn't thinking of me at all. It's like she wants me to come to her out of one of those books."

"Yes, like that fellow by the dam, looking all pale and upset about something," Fritz Pretorius interrupted him. "Yes, I know all that nonsense. And there am I sitting on the rusbank next to her, wearing my best clothes and my veldskoens rubbed smooth with sheep's fat. And she doesn't seem to see me, at all. I don't mind her explaining all about that stuff she reads. I like the sound of her voice. But she doesn't make me feel that I am even a human being to her."

They went on to say that perhaps Jemima didn't want a man who was a human being. Maybe she wanted a lover who reminded her of one of those young men in the poetry books. A young man who wore shining armour. Or jet-black armour. Or even rusty armour. They had all kinds in the different poems that Jemima Oosthuizen explained to her suitors. But where did a young man of the Marico Bushveld come in, in all that?

Lovers came and went. Jemima was never long without a suitor. But she never favoured one above the other – never warming noticeably to anyone. Whatever the qualities were that she sought in a lover – going by the romantic heroes that she read about in old poetry – Jemima never found a Marico lover who fitted in with the things that she read about.

Yes, Gerrit Oosthuizen certainly had a lot of trouble. We even began to feel slightly sorry for him. Here was his daughter who, at a marriageable age, was driving all the young men away from her because of some fantastic ideas that they had put into her head at the finishing-school. Then there were the kaffirs in the Protectorate, who were daily getting more difficult to deal with. And then, finally, there was that new police recruit who was putting in all his time trying to trap Gerrit.

And those who sympathised with Gerrit Oosthuizen also thought it right to blame his daughter on the score of ingratitude. After all, it had cost her father a good deal of money to see Jemima through the finishing-school. He had sent her to the young ladies' seminary in Zeerust in order that she should gain refinement and culture: instead, she had come back talking poetry. Others, again, said that it was her father's lawlessness – which was also, after a fashion, romantic – that had come out in Jemima in that way.

It was on an afternoon when a horseman came riding from over the veld up to her front gate, that Jemima saw the young man that she had read about in olden poems. And she recognised him instantly as her lover. She did not take great note of what he looked like. Nor did she even observe, at first glance, that he was wearing a uniform. All that Jemima Oosthuizen saw very clearly was that, when he came riding up to her from the highway, he was seated on a white horse.

And when she had gone hastily into her bedroom – and had come out again, wearing a pink frock – Jemima hardly understood, at first, the meaning of the young policeman's words when she heard him say, to her father, that he had a warrant for his arrest.

The Picture of Gysbert Jonker

This tobacco-bag, now (Oom Schalk Lourens said, producing a four-ounce linen bag with the picture on it of a leaping blesbuck – the trademark of a well-known tobacco company), well, it is very unusual, the way this tobacco-bag picture fits into the life-story of Gysbert Jonker. I had occasion to think of that only the other day, when at the Zeerust bioscope during the last Nagmaal they showed a film about an English lord who had his portrait painted. And it seemed that after that only the portrait changed, with the years, as the lord grew older and more sinful.

Some of the young people, when they got back from the bioscope, came and called on me, on the kerkplein, and told me what a good film it was. A few of them hinted that I ought also to go to the bioscope, now and again – say, once in two years, or so – to get new ideas for my stories.

Koos Steyn's younger son, Frikkie, even went so far as to say, straight out, that I should go oftener than just once every two years. A good deal oftener. And that I shouldn't see the same film through more than once, either.

"Important things are happening in the world, Oom Schalk," young Frikkie said. "You know, culture and all that. That's why you should go to a film like the one we have just seen. A film with artists in it, and all."

"Yes, artists," another young fellow said. "Like an artist that got pointed out to me last time I was in Johannesburg. With his wide hat and his corduroy trousers, he looked just like a Marico farmer, except that his beard was too wild. We don't grow our beards so long in these parts, anymore, since that new threshing machine with the wide hopper came in. That machine is so quick."

"That is the trouble with your stories, Oom Schalk," Frikkie Steyn continued. "The Boers in them all grow their beards too long. And the uppers of their veldskoens have got an old-fashioned look. Why can't you bring into your next story a young man with a pair of brown shop boots on, and" – hitching his pants up and looking down – "yellow-and-pink striped socks with a – "

"And a waistcoat with long points coming over the top part of the trousers," another young man interrupted him. "And braces with clips that you can make longer or shorter, just as you like."

Anyway, after Theunis Malan had demonstrated to me the difference between a loose and an attached collar, and then couldn't find his stud, and after an ouderling had come past just when another young man was using bad language because he couldn't get his head out through his shirt again – through somebody else having thoughtfully tied the shirt-tails together while the young man was explaining about a new kind of underwear – well, there wasn't much about their new Nagmaal clothes that these young men wanted me to leave out of my next story. And the ouderling, without knowing what was going on, and without trying to find out, even, merely shook his head solemnly as he went past.

And, of course, Frikkie Steyn, just to make sure that I had it right, told the bioscope story of the English lord all over again – all the time that I was filling my pipe from a quarter-pound bag of Magaliesberg tobacco; the sort with the picture of the high-bounding blesbuck on it.

So I thought, well, maybe Gysbert was not an English lord. But I could remember the time when his portrait, painted in the most beautiful colours, hung in his voorkamer. And I also thought of the way in which Gysbert's portrait was on display on every railway platform and in every Indian shop in the country. And almost until the very end the portrait remained unchanged. It was only Gysbert Jonker who, despite all his efforts, altered with the years. But when the portrait did eventually change, it was a much more incredible transformation than anything that could have happened to the portrait of that lord in the bioscope story.

It was while we were sitting in the Indian store at Ramoutsa, drinking coffee and waiting for the afternoon to get cool enough for us to be able to drive back home by mule- and donkey-cart, that we first noticed the resemblance.

Our conversation was, as usual, of an edifying character. We spoke about how sensible we were to go on sitting in the Indian store, hour after hour, like that, and drinking coffee, instead of driving out in the hot sun, and running the risk of getting sunstroke. Later on, when some clouds came up, we were even more glad that we had not ventured out in our open carts, because everybody knows that the worst kind of sunstroke is what you get when the sun shines on to the back of your head through the clouds.

Of course, there were other forms of conveyance, such as Cape-carts, we said. But that sort of thing only undermined you. Naturally, we did not wish to be undermined. We spoke about how the younger generation was losing its self-reliance through – and we started naming some of the things we saw on the shelves around us. Gramophones, we said. And paraffin candles in packets, we said, instead of making our own. And tubes with white grease that you squeeze at the end to polish your plates and spoons with, one of us said. No, it was to brush your teeth with, somebody else interrupted him. And we said that, well, whatever it was for, it was undermining. And we said that our own generation was being sapped, also.

After we had asked the Indian behind the counter to stand to one side, so that we could see better how we were being undermined, Hans Bekker pointed to a shelf holding tins of coffee. "Formerly we burnt and ground our own coffee," Hans Bekker said. "Today – "

"Before I could walk," Andries Claassens said, "I used to shred my own tobacco from a black roll. I could cut up plug tobacco for my pipe before I could sharpen a slate-pencil. But now I have to sit with this little bag – "

I don't know who made the following observation, but we laughed at it for a long time. We looked back from Andries Claassens's tobacco-bag to the shelf on which dozens of similar bags were displayed. On each was the picture of a farmer with a black beard and a red-and-yellow checked shirt; and in his right hand, which was raised level with his shoulders, he held, elegantly if somewhat stiffly, a pipe. Perhaps you remember that picture, which did not appear only on the tobacco-bags, but was reproduced, also, in the newspapers, and stood on oblong metal sheets, enamelled in bright colours, in front of every store.

When our attention had been drawn to it, we saw the resemblance very clearly. In respect of both his features and his expression, the farmer on the tobacco-bag was almost the exact image of Gysbert Jonker. Gysbert's beard was not so neatly trimmed, and his eyebrows were straighter; also, his mouth considerably larger than the man's on the picture. But in every other way – taking into consideration the difference in their dress – the likeness was astonishing.

Gysbert Jonker was there, in the Indian store, with us, when we made the discovery. He seemed very much interested.

"You will now have to push your ears in under the sweatband of your hat, in the city fashion," Hans Bekker said to Gysbert. "You can't have them bent anymore."

"And you will now have to hold your pipe up in the air, next to your shoulder, when you walk behind the plough," Andries Claassens added, "in your riding-breeches and leggings."

We were more than a little surprised at Gysbert's answer.

"It is absurd to think that I could do farm-work in that rig-out," he replied. "But on Sundays, and some evenings after work, I shall wear riding-pants and top-boots. And it's a queer thing, but I have always wanted a shirt with red-and-yellow checks. In any case, it's the least I can do, in view of the fact that this tobacco company has honoured the Marico by making use of the portrait of the district's most progressive cattle farmer in this way. I suppose the tobacco firm selected me for this purpose because of the improvements I made to my cement-dip last year."

Gysbert Jonker added that next year he intended erecting another barbed-wire camp on the other side of the dam, and that he could bring this to the notice of the tobacco company as well.

We suddenly found that we had nothing more to say. And we were so taken aback at the way Gysbert responded to the purely accidental circumstance of his resembling the man in the picture that we were quite unable to laugh about it, even.

And I am sure that I was not the only Marico farmer, driving back home later that afternoon over the dusty road through the camel-thorns, who reflected earnestly on the nature (and dangers) of sunstroke.

After a while, however, we got used to the change that had taken place in Gysbert Jonker's soul.

Consequently, with the passage of time, there was less and less said about the gorgeously coloured shirts that Gysbert Jonker wore on Sundays, when he strolled about the front part of his homestead in riding breeches and gaiters, apparently carefree and at ease, except that he held his pipe high up near his shoulder, somewhat stiffly. In time, too, the ouderling ceased calling on Gysbert in order to dissuade him from going about dressed as a tobacco advertisement on Sundays – a practice that the ouderling regarded as a desecration of the Sabbath.

In spite of everything, we had to admit that Gysbert Jonker had succeeded to a remarkable degree in imitating his portrait – especially when he started shaving the sides of his eyebrows to make them look more curved, and when he had cultivated a smile that wrinkled up his left cheek, halfway to his ear. And he used to smile carefully, almost as though he was afraid that some of the enamel would chip off him.

Jonker on one occasion announced to a number of acquaintances at a meeting of the Dwarsberg debating society: "Look at this shirt I have got on, for instance. Just feel the quality of it, and then compare it with the shirt on your tobacco-bag. I had my photo taken last month in Zeerust, in these clothes. I sent the photograph to the head office of the tobacco company in Johannesburg – and would you believe it? The tobacco people sent me by the following railway-lorry, one of those life-sized enamelled pictures of myself painted on a sheet of iron. You know, the kind that you see on stations and in front of shops. I nailed it to the wall of my voorkamer."

Gysbert kept up this foolishness for a number of years. And it was, of course, this particular characteristic of his that we admired. We could see from this that he was a real Afrikaner, as obstinate as the Transvaal turf-soil. Even when, with the years, it became difficult for him to compete successfully with his portrait that did not age, so that he had to resort to artificial aids to keep his hair and beard black – then we did not laugh about it. We even sympathised with him in his hopeless struggle against the onslaughts of time. And we noticed that, the older Gysbert Jonker got, the more youthful his shirt seemed.

In the end, Gysbert Jonker had had to hands-up, of course. But he gave in only after his portrait had changed. And it was so stupendous a change that it was beyond the capacity even of Gysbert to try to follow suit. One day suddenly – without any kind of warning from the tobacco firm – we noticed, when we were again in the Indian store at Ramoutsa, that the picture of the farmer in riding pants had disappeared from the tobacco-bags. Just like that. The farmer was replaced with the picture of the leaping blesbuck that you see on this bag, here. Afterwards, the blesbuck took the place of the riding-pants farmer on the enamelled iron sheets as well.

Meanwhile, however, when it dawned on us that the tobacco company was busy changing its advertisement, we made many carefully considered remarks about Gysbert Jonker. We said that he would now, in his old age, have to start practising the high-jump, in order to be able to resemble his new portrait. We also said that he would now have to paint his belly white, like the blesbuck's. We also expressed the hope that a leopard wouldn't catch Gysbert Jonker when he walked about the veld on a Sunday morning, dressed up like his new portrait.

Nevertheless, I had the feeling that Gysbert Jonker did not altogether regret the fact that his portrait had been unrecognisably changed. For one thing, he was now relieved of the strain of having all the time to live up to the opinion that the tobacco company had formed of him.

And although he removed the enamelled portrait from the wall of his voorkamer, and used it to repair a hole in the pigsty, and although he wore his gaudily coloured shirts every day, now, and while doing the roughest kind of work, just so as to get rid of them – yet there were times, when I looked at Gysbert Jonker, that my thoughts were carried right back to the past. Most often this would happen when he was smoking. To the end, he retained something of his enamelled way of holding his pipe – his hand raised almost level with his shoulder, elegantly, but just a shade stiffly.

Some years later, when Gysbert Jonker was engaged in wearing out the last of his red-and-yellow checked shirts, I came across him at the back of his pigsty. He was standing near the spot where he had replaced a damaged sheet of corrugated iron with his tobacco-advertisement portrait.

And it struck me that in some mysterious way, Gysbert Jonker had again caught up with his portrait. For they looked equally shabby and dilapidated, then, the portrait and Gysbert Jonker. They seemed to have become equally sullied – through the years and through sin. And so I turned away quickly from that rusted sheet of iron, with the picture on it of that farmer with his battered pipe, and his beard that was now greying and unkempt. And his shirt that looked as patched as Gysbert Jonker's own. And his eyes that had grown as wistful.

Treasure Trove

It is queer (Oom Schalk Lourens said), about treasure hunting. You can actually find the treasure, and through ignorance, or through forgetting to look, at the moment when you have got it, you can let it slip through your fingers like sand. Take Namaqualand, for instance. That part where all the diamonds are lying around, waiting to be picked up. Now they have got it all fenced in, and there are hundreds of police patrolling what we thought, in those days, was just a piece of desert. I remember the last time I trekked through that part of the country, which I took to be an ungodly stretch of sandy waste. But if I had known that I was travelling through thousands of miles of diamond mine, I don't think I would have hurried so much. And that area wouldn't have seemed so very ungodly, either.

I made the last part of the journey on foot. And you know how it is when you are walking through the sand; how you have to stop every so often to sit down and shake out your boots. I get quite a sick feeling, even now, when I think that I never once looked to see what I was shaking out. You hear of a person allowing a fortune to slip through his fingers. But it is much sadder if he lets it trickle away through between the leather of his veldskoens.

Anyway, when the talk comes round to fortunes, and so on, I always call to mind the somewhat singular search that went on, for the better part of a Bushveld summer, on Jan Slabbert's farm. We all said, afterwards, that Jan Slabbert should have known better, at his age and experience, than to have allowed a stranger like that callow young Hendrik Buys, on the strength of a few lines drawn on a piece of wrapping paper, to come along and start up so much foolishness.

Jan Slabbert was very mysterious about the whole thing, at first. He introduced Hendrik Buys to us as "a young man from the Cape who is having a look over my farm." These words of Jan Slabbert's did not, however, reveal to us much that we did not already know. Indeed, I had on more than one occasion come across Hendrik Buys, unexpectedly and from behind, when he was quite clearly engaged in looking over Jan Slabbert's farm. He had even got down on his hands and knees to look it over better.

But in the end, after several neighbours had unexpectedly come across Jan Slabbert in the same way, he admitted that they were conducting a search for hidden treasure.

"I suppose, because it's hidden treasure, Jan Slabbert thinks that it has got to be kept hidden from us, also," Jurie Bekker said one day when several of us were sitting in his post office.

"It's a treasure consisting of gold coins and jewels that were buried on Jan Slabbert's farm many years ago," Neels Erasmus, who was a church elder, explained. "I called on Jan Slabbert – not because I was inquisitive about the treasure, of course – but in connection with something of a theological character that happened at the last Nagmaal, and Jan Slabbert and Hendrik Buys were both out. They were on the veld."

"On their hands and knees," Jurie Bekker said.

The ouderling went on to tell us that Jan Slabbert's daughter, Susannah, had said that a piece of the map which that young fellow, Buys, had brought with him from the Cape, was missing, with the result that they were having difficulty in locating the spot marked with a cross.

"It's always like that with a map of a place where there is buried treasure," Jurie Bekker said. "You follow a lot of directions, until you come to an old tree or an old grave or an old forked road with cobwebs on it, and then you have to take a hundred paces to the west, and then there's something missing – "

Neels Erasmus, the ouderling, said *he* was talking to Susannah, and his voice sounded kind of rasping. He always liked to be the first with the news. But Jurie Bekker was able to assure us that he had just guessed those details. Every treasure-hunt map was like that, he repeated.

"Well, you got it pretty right," Neels Erasmus said. "There *is* an old tree in it, and an old forked road and an old grave, I think, and also a pair of men's underpants – the long kind. The underpants seem to have been the oldest clue of the whole lot. And it was the underpants that convinced Jan Slabbert that the map was genuine. He was doubtful about it, until then."

The ouderling went on to say that where this map also differed from the usual run of treasure-trove maps was that you didn't have to pace off one hundred yards to the west in the last stage of trying to locate the spot.

"Instead," he explained, "you've got to crawl on your hands and knees for I don't know how far. You see, the treasure was buried at night. And the men that buried it crawled through the bush on hands and knees for the last part of the way."

We said that from the positions in which we had often seen Jan

Slabbert and Hendrik Buys of late, it was clear that they were also on the last part of their search.

Andries Prinsloo, a young man who had all this while been sitting in a corner on a low riempiestoel, and had until then taken no part in the conversation, suddenly remarked to Neels Erasmus (and he cleared his throat nervously as he spoke), that it seemed to him as though the ouderling "and – and Susannah – er – had quite a lot to say to each other." Perhaps it was because he was respectful of our company that Andries Prinsloo spoke so diffidently.

At all events, Andries Prinsloo's remark started us off saying all kinds of things of an improving nature.

"Yes," I said to Neels Erasmus, "I wonder what your wife would say if she knew that you went to call at Jan Slabbert's house when only his daughter, Susannah, was at home."

"You went in the morning, because you knew that Jan Slabbert and Hendrik Buys would be outside, then, creeping through the wag-'n-bietjie thorns," Jurie Bekker said. "The afternoons, of course, they keep free for creeping through the haakdoring thorns."

"And what will your wife say if she knew of the subjects you discussed with Susannah?" I asked.

"Yes, all those intimate things," Jurie Bekker continued. "Like about that pair of old underpants. How could you talk to a young, innocent girl like Susannah about those awful old underp – "

Jurie Bekker spluttered so much that he couldn't get the word out. Then we both broke into loud guffaws. And in the midst of all this laughter, Andries Prinsloo went out very quietly, almost as though he didn't want to disturb us. It seemed that that young fellow had so much respect for our company that he did not wish to take part in anything that might resemble unseemly mirth. And we did not feel like laughing anymore, either, somehow, after he had left.

When we again discussed Jan Slabbert's affairs in the post office, the treasure hunt had reached the stage where a gang of kaffirs, under the supervision of the two white men, went from place to place on the farm, digging holes. In some places they even dug tunnels. They found nothing. We said that it would only be somebody like Jan Slabbert, who was already the richest man in the whole of the Northern Transvaal, that would get all worked up over the prospect of unearthing buried treasure.

"Jan Slabbert has given Hendrik Buys a contract," Neels Erasmus, the ouderling, said. "I learnt about it when I went there in connection with something of an ecclesiastical nature that happened at the Nagmaal before last. They will split whatever treasure they find. Jan Slabbert will get two-thirds and Hendrik Buys one-third."

We said that it sounded a sinful arrangement, somehow. We also spoke much about what it said in the Good Book about treasures in heaven that the moth could not corrupt. That was after Neels Erasmus had said that there was no chance of the treasure having been buried on some neighbour's farm, instead, by mistake.

"Actually, according to the map," the ouderling said, "it would appear that the treasure is buried right in the middle of Jan Slabbert's farm, somewhere. Just about where his house is."

"If Hendrik Buys has got any sense," Jurie Bekker said, "he would drive a tunnel right under Jan Slabbert's house, and as far as under his bedroom. If the tunnel came out under Jan Slabbert's bed, where he keeps that iron chest of his – well, even if Hendrik Buys is allowed to take only one-third of what is in there, it will still be something."

We then said that perhaps that was the treasure that was marked on Hendrik Buys's map with a cross, but that they hadn't guessed it yet.

That gave me an idea. I asked how Jan Slabbert's daughter, Susannah, was taking all those irregular carryings-on on the farm. The ouderling moved the winking muscle of his left eye in a peculiar way.

"The moment Hendrik Buys came into the house I understood it all clearly," he said. "Susannah's face got all lit up as she kind of skipped into the kitchen to make fresh coffee. But Hendrik Buys was too wrapped up in the treasure-hunt business to notice, even. What a pity – a nice girl like that, and all."

It seemed that that well-behaved young fellow, Andries Prinsloo, who always took the same place in the corner, was getting more respect for our company than ever. Because, this time, when he slipped out of the post office – and it was just about at that moment, too – he appeared actually to be walking on tiptoe.

Well, I didn't come across Jan Slabbert and Hendrik Buys again until about the time when they had finally decided to abandon the search. They had quarrelled quite often, too, by then. They would be on quite friendly terms when they showed the kaffirs where to start digging another hole. But by the time the hole was very wide, and about ten foot deep, in blue slate, they would start quarrelling.

The funny part of it all was that Hendrik Buys remained optimistic about the treasure right through, and he wouldn't have given up, either, if in the course of their last quarrel Jan Slabbert had not decided the matter for him, bundling him on to the Government lorry back to Zeerust, after kicking him.

The quarrel had to do with a hole eighteen foot deep, in gneiss.

But on that last occasion on which I saw them together in the voorkamer, Jan Slabbert and his daughter, Susannah, and Hendrik Buys, it seemed to me that Hendrik Buys was still very hopeful.

"There are lots of parts of the farm that I haven't crawled through yet," Hendrik Buys explained. "Likely places, according to the map, such as the pigsty. I have not yet crept through the pigsty. I must remember that for tomorrow. You see, the men who buried the treasure crept for the last part of the way through the bush in the dark." Hendrik Buys paused. It was clear that an idea had struck him. "Do you think it possible," he asked, excitedly, "that they might have crawled through the bush *backwards* – you know, in the dark? That is something that I had not thought of until this moment. What do you say, Oom Jan, tomorrow you and I go and creep backwards, in the direction of the pigsty?"

Jan Slabbert did not answer. And Susannah's efforts at keeping the conversation going made the situation seem all the more awkward. I felt sorry for her. It was a relief to us all when Neels Erasmus, the ouderling, arrived at the front door just then. He had come to see Jan Slabbert in connection with something of an apostolic description that might happen at the forthcoming Nagmaal.

I never saw Hendrik Buys again, but I did think of him quite a number of times afterwards, particularly on the occasion of Susannah Slabbert's wedding. And I wondered, in the course of his treasure hunting, how much Hendrik Buys had possibly let slip through his fingers like sand. That was when the ceremony was over, and a couple of men among the wedding guests were discharging their Mausers into the air – welcoming the bride as she was being lifted down from the Cape-cart by the quiet-mannered young fellow, Andries Prinsloo. He seemed more subdued than ever, now, as a bridegroom.

And so I understood then about the distracted air which Andries Prinsloo had worn throughout that feverish time of the great Bushveld treasure hunt; that it was in reality the half-dazed look of a man who had unearthed a pot of gold at the foot of the rainbow.

The Ferreira Millions

Marthinus Taljaard lived in a house that his grandfather had built on the slope of a koppie in the Dwarsberge (Oom Schalk Lourens said). It was a big, rambling house with more rooms than what Marthinus Taljaard needed for just his daughter, Rosina, and himself. Marthinus Taljaard was known as the richest man in the whole of the Dwarsberge. It was these two circumstances that led to the koppie around his house becoming hollowed out with tunnels like the nest of a white ant.

Only a man who, like Marthinus Taljaard, already had more possessions in cattle and money than he knew what to do with, would still want more. That was why he listened to the story that Giel Bothma came all the way from Johannesburg to tell him about the Ferreira millions.

Of course, any Marico farmer would have been interested to hear what a young man in city clothes had to say, talking fast, about the meaning of a piece of yellow paper with lines and words on it, that he held in his hand. If Giel Bothma had come to me in that way, I would have listened to him, also. We would have sat on the stoep, drinking coffee. And I would have told him that it was a good story. I would also have shown him, if he was a young man willing to learn, how he could improve on it. Furthermore, I would have told him a few stories of my own, by way of guidance to him as to how to tell a story.

But towards milking time I would have to leave that young man sitting on the stoep, the while I went out to see what was happening in the cattle-kraal.

That was where Marthinus Taljaard, because he was the wealthiest man in the Dwarsberge, was different. He listened to Giel Bothma's story about the Ferreira millions from the early part of the forenoon onwards. He listened with his mouth open. And when it came to milking time, he invited Giel Bothma over to the kraal with him, with Giel Bothma still talking. And when it came to the time for feeding the pigs, Giel Bothma helped to carry a heavy bucket of swill to the troughs, without seeming to notice the looks of surprise on the faces of the Bechuana farm labourers.

A little later, when Giel Bothma saw what the leaking bucket of swill had done to the legs of his smoothly pressed trousers, he spoke a lot more. And what he used were not just all city words, either.

Anyway, the result of Giel Bothma's visit from Johannesburg was that he convinced Marthinus Taljaard, by means of the words and lines on that bit of yellow paper, that the Ferreira millions, a treasure comprised of gold and diamonds and elephant tusks, was buried on his farm.

We in the Marico had, needless to say, never heard of the Ferreira million before. We knew only that Ferreira was a good Afrikaner name. And we often sang that old song, "Vat jou goed en trek, Ferreira" – meaning to journey northwards out of the Cape to get away from English rule. Moreover, there was the Hans Ferreira family. They were Doppers and lived near Enzelsberg. But when you saw Hans Ferreira at the Indian store at Ramoutsa, lifting a few sheep-skins out of his donkey-cart and trying to exchange them for coffee and sugar, then you could not help greeting with a certain measure of amusement the idea conveyed by the words, 'Ferreira millions.'

These were the matters that we discussed one midday while we were sitting around in Jurie Steyn's post office, waiting for our letters from Zeerust.

Marthinus Taljaard and his daughter, Rosina, had come to the post office, leaving Giel Bothma alone on the farm to work out, with the help of his yellowed map and the kaffirs, the place where to dig the tunnel.

"This map with the Ferreira millions in gold and diamonds and elephant tusks," Marthinus Taljaard said, pompously, sitting forward on Jurie Steyn's riempiestoel, "was made many years ago – before my grandfather's time, even. That's why it is so yellow. Giel Bothma got hold of it just by accident. And the map shows clearly that the Portuguese explorer, Ferreira, buried his treasure somewhere in that koppie in the middle of my farm."

"Anyway, that piece of paper is yellow enough," Jurie Steyn said with a slight sneer. "That paper is yellower than the iron pyrites that a prospector found at Witfontein, so it must be gold, all right. And I can also see that it is gold, from the way you hang on to it."

Several of us laughed, then.

"But I can't imagine there being such a thing as the Ferreira millions," Stephanus van Tonder said, expressing what we all felt. "Not if you think that Hans Ferreira's wife went to the last Nagmaal with a mimosa thorn holding up her skirt because they didn't have a safety-pin in the house."

Marthinus Taljaard explained to us where we were wrong.

"The treasure was buried on my farm very long ago," Marthinus Taljaard said, "long before there were any white people in the Transvaal. It was the treasure that the Portuguese explorer, Ferreira, stole from the Mtosas. Maybe that Portuguese explorer was the ancestor of Hans Ferreira. I don't know. But I am talking about very long ago, before the Ferreiras were Afrikaners, but were just Portuguese. I am talking of *very* long ago."

We told Marthinus Taljaard that he had better not make wild statements like that in Hans Ferreira's hearing. Hans Ferreira was a Dopper and quick-tempered. And even though he had to trade sheep-skins for coffee and sugar, we said, not being able to wait to change the skins into money first, he would nevertheless go many miles out of his way with a sjambok to look for a man who spoke of him as a Portuguese.

And no matter how long ago, either, we added.

Marthinus Taljaard sat up even straighter on the riempiestoel then.

By way of changing the conversation, Jurie Steyn asked Marthinus how he knew for certain that it was his farm on which the treasure was buried.

Marthinus Taljaard said that that part of the map was very clear.

"The site of the treasure, marked with a cross, is twelve thousand Cape feet north of Abjaterskop, in a straight line," he said, "so that's almost in the exact middle of my farm."

He went on to explain, wistfully, that that was about the only part of the map that was in a straight line.

"It's all in Cape roods and Cape ells, like it has on the back of the school exercise books," Marthinus Taljaard's daughter, Rosina, went on to tell us. "That's what makes it so hard for Mr Bothma to work out the Ferreira map. We sometimes sit up quite late at night, working out sums."

After Marthinus Taljaard and Rosina had left, we said that young Giel Bothma must be pretty slow for a young man. Sitting up late at night with an attractive girl like Rosina Taljaard, and being able to think of nothing better to do than working out sums.

We also said it was funny that that first Ferreira should have filled up his treasure map with Cape measurements, when the later Ferreiras were in so much of a hurry to trek away from anything that even looked like the Cape.

In the months that followed there was a great deal of activity on Marthinus Taljaard's farm. I didn't go over there myself, but other farmers had passed that way, driving slowly in their mule-carts down the Government Road and trying to see all they could without appearing inquisitive. From them I learnt that a large number of tunnels had been dug into the side of a hill on which the Taljaard farmhouse stood.

During those months, also, several of Marthinus Taljaard's Bechuanas left him and came to work for me. That new kind of work on Baas Taljaard's farm was too hard, one of them told me, brushing red soil off his elbow. He also said that Baas Taljaard was unappreciative of their best efforts at digging holes into the side of the koppie. And each time a hole came to an end, and there was no gold in it, or diamonds or elephant teeth, then Baas Taljaard would take a kick at whatever native was nearest.

"He kicked me as though it was my fault that there was no gold there," another Bechuana said to me with a grin, "instead of blaming it on that yellow paper with the writing on it."

The Bechuana said that on a subsequent occasion, when there was no gold at the end of a tunnel that was particularly wide and long, Marthinus Taljaard ran a few yards (Cape yards, I supposed), and took a kick at Giel Bothma.

No doubt Baas Taljaard did that by mistake, the Bechuana added, his grin almost as wide as one of those tunnels.

More months passed before I again saw Marthinus Taljaard and his daughter in Jurie Steyn's post office. Marthinus was saying that they were now digging a tunnel that he was sure was the right one.

"It points straight at my house," he said, "and where it comes up, there we'll find the treasure. We have now worked out from the map that the tunnel should go up, at the end. That wasn't clear before, because there is something missing – "

"Yes, the treasure," Jurie Steyn said, winking at Stephanus van Tonder.

"No," Rosina interjected, flushing. "There is a corner missing from the map. That bit of the map remained between the thumb and forefinger of the man in the bar when he gave it to Giel Bothma."

"We only found out afterwards that Giel Bothma had that map given to him by crooks in a bar," Marthinus Taljaard said. "If I had known about that from the start, I don't know if I would have been so keen about it. Why I listened was because Giel Bothma was so well dressed, in city clothes, and all."

Marthinus Taljaard stirred his coffee.

"But he isn't anymore," he resumed, reflectively. "Not well dressed, I mean. You should have seen how his suit looked after the first week of tunnelling."

We had quite a lot to say after Marthinus Taljaard and Rosina left.

"Crooks in a bar," Stephanus van Tonder snorted. "It's all clear to me, now. That tunnel is going to come up right under Marthinus Taljaard's bed, where he keeps his money in that tamboetie chest. I am sure that map has got nothing to do with the Ferreira treasure at all. But it seems a pretty good map of the Taljaard treasure."

We also said that it was a very peculiar way that that crook had of *giving* Giel Bothma the map. With one corner of it remaining in his hand. It certainly looked as though Giel Bothma must have pulled on it, a little.

We never found out how much truth there was in our speculations. For we learnt some time later that Giel Bothma did get hold of the Taljaard fortune, after all. He got it by marrying Rosina. And that last tunnel did come up under a part of Marthinus Taljaard's rambling old house, built on the side of the koppie. It came up at the end of a long passage, right in front of the door of Rosina Taljaard's bedroom.

Unto Dust

I have noticed that when a young man or woman dies, people get the feeling that there is something beautiful and touching in the event, and that it is different from the death of an old person. In the thought, say, of a girl of twenty sinking into an untimely grave, there is a sweet wistfulness that makes people talk all kinds of romantic words. She died, they say, young, she that was so full of life and so fair. She was a flower that withered before it bloomed, they say, and it all seems so fitting and beautiful that there is a good deal of resentment, at the funeral, over the crude questions that a couple of men in plain clothes from the landdrost's office are asking about cattle-dip.

But when you have grown old, nobody is very much interested in the manner of your dying. Nobody except you yourself, that is. And I think that your past life has got a lot to do with the way you feel when you get near the end of your days. I remember how, when he was lying on his death-bed, Andries Wessels kept on telling us that it was because of the blameless path he had trodden from his earliest years that he could compose himself in peace to lay down his burdens. And I certainly never saw a man breathe his last more tranquilly, seeing that right up to the end he kept on murmuring to us how happy he was, with heavenly hosts and invisible choirs of angels all around him.

Just before he died, he told us that the angels had even become visible. They were medium-sized angels, he said, and they had cloven hoofs and carried forks. It was obvious that Andries Wessels's ideas were getting a bit confused by then, but all the same I never saw a man die in a more hallowed sort of calm.

Once, during the malaria season in the Eastern Transvaal, it seemed to me, when I was in a high fever and like to die, that the whole world was a big burial-ground. I thought it was the earth itself that was a graveyard, and not just those little fenced-in bits of land dotted with tombstones, in the shade of a Western Province oak-tree or by the side of a Transvaal koppie. This was a nightmare that worried me a great deal, and so I was very glad, when I recovered from the fever, to think that we Boers had properly marked-out places on our farms for white people to be laid to rest in, in a civilised Christian way, instead of having to be buried just anyhow, along with a dead wild-cat, maybe, or a Bushman with a clay pot, and things.

When I mentioned this to my friend, Stoffel Oosthuizen, who was in the Low Country with me at the time, he agreed with me wholeheartedly. There were people who talked in a high-flown way of death as the great leveller, he said, and those high-flown people also declared that everyone was made kin by death. He would still like to see those things proved, Stoffel Oosthuizen said. After all, that was one of the reasons why the Boers had trekked away into the Transvaal and the Free State, he said, because the British Government wanted to give the vote to any Cape Coloured person walking about with a kroes head and big cracks in his feet.

The first time he heard that sort of talk about death coming to all of us alike, and making us all equal, Stoffel Oosthuizen's suspicions were aroused. It sounded like out of a speech made by one of those liberal Cape politicians, he explained.

I found something very comforting in Stoffel Oosthuizen's words.

Then, to illustrate his contention, Stoffel Oosthuizen told me a story of an incident that took place in a bygone Transvaal kaffir war. I don't know whether he told the story incorrectly, or whether it was just that kind of a story, but, by the time he had finished, all my uncertainties had, I discovered, come back to me.

"You can go and look at Hans Welman's tombstone any time you are at Nietverdiend," Stoffel Oosthuizen said. "The slab of red sandstone is weathered by now, of course, seeing how long ago it all happened. But the inscription is still legible. I was with Hans Welman on that morning when he fell. Our commando had been ambushed by the kaffirs and was retreating. I could do nothing for Hans Welman. Once, when I looked round, I saw a tall kaffir bending over him and plunging an assegai into him. Shortly afterwards I saw the kaffir stripping the clothes off Hans Welman. A yellow kaffir dog was yelping excitedly around his black master. Although I was in grave danger myself, with several dozen kaffirs making straight for me on foot through the bush, the fury I felt at the sight of what that tall kaffir was doing made me hazard a last shot. Reining in my horse, and taking what aim I could under the circumstances, I pressed the trigger. My luck was in. I saw the kaffir fall forward beside the naked body of Hans Welman. Then I set spurs to my horse and galloped off at full speed, with the foremost of my pursuers already almost upon me. The last I saw was that yellow dog bounding up to his master – whom I had wounded mortally, as we were to discover later.

"As you know, that kaffir war dragged on for a long time. There were few pitched battles. Mainly, what took place were bush skirmishes, like the one in which Hans Welman lost his life.

"After about six months, quiet of a sort was restored to the Marico and Zoutpansberg Districts. Then the day came when I went out, in company of a handful of other burghers, to fetch in the remains of Hans Welman, at his widow's request, for burial in the little cemetery plot on the farm. We took a coffin with us on a Cape-cart.

"We located the scene of the skirmish without difficulty. Indeed, Hans Welman had been killed not very far from his own farm, which had been temporarily abandoned, together with the other farms in that part, during the time that the trouble with the kaffirs had lasted. We drove up to the spot where I remembered having seen Hans Welman lying dead on the ground, with the tall kaffir next to him. From a distance I again saw that yellow dog. He slipped away into the bush at our approach. I could not help feeling that there was something rather stirring about that beast's fidelity, even though it was bestowed on a dead kaffir.

"We were now confronted with a queer situation. We found that what was left of Hans Welman and the kaffir consisted of little more than pieces of sun-dried flesh and the dismembered fragments of bleached skeletons. The sun and wild animals and birds of prey had done their work. There was a heap of human bones, with here and there leathery strips of blackened flesh. But we could not tell which was the white man and which the kaffir. To make it still more confusing, a lot of bones were missing altogether, having no doubt been dragged away by wild animals into their lairs in the bush. Another thing was that Hans Welman and that kaffir had been just about the same size."

Stoffel Oosthuizen paused in his narrative, and I let my imagination dwell for a moment on that situation. And I realised just how those Boers must have felt about it: about the thought of bringing the remains of a Transvaal burgher home to his widow for Christian burial, and perhaps having a lot of kaffir bones mixed up with the burgher – lying with him in the same tomb on which the mauve petals from the oleander overhead would fall.

"I remember one of our party saying that that was the worst of these kaffir wars," Stoffel Oosthuizen continued. "If it had been a war against the English, and part of a dead Englishman had got lifted into that coffin by mistake, it wouldn't have mattered so much," he said.

There seemed to me in this story to be something as strange as the African veld.

Stoffel Oosthuizen said that the little party of Boers spent almost a whole afternoon with the remains in order to try to get the white man sorted out from the kaffir. By the evening they had laid all they could find of what seemed like Hans Welman's bones in the coffin in the Cape-cart. The rest of the bones and flesh they buried on the spot.

Stoffel Oosthuizen added that, no matter what the difference in the colour of their skin had been, it was impossible to say that the kaffir's bones were less white than Hans Welman's. Nor was it possible to say that the kaffir's sun-dried flesh was any blacker than the white man's. Alive, you couldn't go wrong in distinguishing between a white man and a kaffir. Dead, you had great difficulty in telling them apart.

"Naturally, we burghers felt very bitter about this whole affair," Stoffel Oosthuizen said, "and our resentment was something that we couldn't explain, quite. Afterwards, several other men who were there that day told me that they had the same feelings of suppressed anger that I did. They wanted somebody – just once – to make a remark such as 'in death they were not divided.' Then you would have seen an outburst, all right. Nobody did say anything like that, however. We all knew better. Two days later a funeral service was conducted in the little cemetery on the Welman farm, and shortly afterwards the sandstone memorial was erected that you can still see there."

That was the story Stoffel Oosthuizen told me after I had recovered from the fever. It was a story that, as I have said, had in it features as strange as the African veld. But it brought me no peace in my broodings after that attack of malaria. Especially when Stoffel Oosthuizen spoke of how he had occasion, one clear night when the stars shone, to pass that quiet graveyard on the Welman farm. Something leapt up from the mound beside the sandstone slab. It gave him quite a turn, Stoffel Oosthuizen said, for the third time – and in that way – to come across that yellow kaffir dog.

Bush Telegraph

*B*oom – boom – boom – *boom* – boom – boom – those kaffir drums (Oom Schalk Lourens said). There they go again. There must be a big beer drink being held in those Mtosa huts in the vlakte. Boom – *boom* – boom – boom. Yes, it sounds like a good party, all right.

Of course, that's about all the kaffirs use their drums for, these days – to summon the neighbours to a dance. But there was a time when the sound of the drums travelled from one end of Africa to the other.

In the old days the drum-men would receive and send messages that went from village to village and across thick bush and by deserts, and it made no difference what languages were spoken by the various tribes, either. The drum-men would know what a message meant, no matter where it came from.

The drum-man was taught his work from boyhood. And sometimes when a drum-man got a message to say that a cattle-raiding impi sent out by the chief was on its way back without cattle, and running quite fast – some of the fatter indunas throwing away their spears as they were running – then the chief would as likely as not be ungrateful about the message, and would have the drum-man taken around the corner and stoned, as though it was the drum-man's fault.

Afterwards, however, when we white men brought the telegraph up through these parts on the copper wires, there wasn't any more need for the kaffir drums.

I remember the last drum-man they had at the Mtosa huts outside Ramoutsa. His name was Mosigo. He was very old and his face was wrinkled. I often thought that those wrinkles looked like the kaffir footpaths that go twisting across the length and breadth of Africa, and that you can follow for mile after mile and day after day, and that never come to an end. And I would think how the messages that Mosigo received on his drum would come from somewhere along the furthest paths that the kaffirs followed across Africa, getting foot-sore on the way, and that were like the wrinkles on Mosigo's face.

"The drum is better than the copper wire that you white men bring up on long poles across the veld," Mosigo said to me on one occasion.

He was sitting in front of his hut and was tapping on his drum that went *boom* – boom – boom – boom – *boom* – boom. (Just like the way you hear that drum going down there in the vlakte, now.)

Far away it seemed as though other drums were taking up and repeating Mosigo's pattern of drum-sounds. Or it may be that what you heard, coming from the distant koppies, were only echoes.

"I don't need copper wires for my drum's messages," Mosigo went on. "Or long poles with rows of little white medicine bottles on them, either."

Now, this talk that I had with Mosigo took place very long ago. It happened soon after the first telegraph office was opened at Nietverdiend. And so when I went to Nietverdiend a few days later, it was natural that I should have mentioned to a few of my Bushveld neighbours at the post office what Mosigo had said.

I was not surprised to find that those farmers were in the main in agreement with Mosigo's remarks. Gysbert van Tonder said it was well known how ignorant the kaffirs were, but there were also some things that the kaffirs did have more understanding of than white men.

Then Gysbert van Tonder told us about the time when he had gone with his brother, 'Rooi', to hunt elephants far up into Portuguese territory. And wherever they went, he and his brother 'Rooi', the kaffirs knew beforehand of their coming, by means of the drums.

"I tried to get some of the drum-men to explain to me what the different sounds they made on the drums meant," Gysbert van Tonder said. "But that again shows you the really ignorant side of the kaffir. Those drum-men just couldn't get me to understand the first thing of what they were wanting to teach me. And it wasn't that they didn't try, mind you. Indeed, some of the drum-men were very patient about it. They would explain over and over again. But I just couldn't grasp it. They were so ignorant, I mean."

Gysbert van Tonder went on to say that afterwards, through having heard that same message tapped out so often, he grew to recognise the kind of taps that meant that his brother, 'Rooi', had killed an elephant. And then the day came when an elephant killed his brother, 'Rooi.' And Gysbert van Tonder listened carefully to the drums. And it was the same message as always, he said. Only, it was the other way around.

As I have told you, the telegraph had only recently come up as far as Nietverdiend. And because we had no newspaper here in those days, the telegraph-operator, who was a young fellow without much sense, had arranged with a friend in the Pretoria head office to send him short items of news which he pinned on the wall inside the post office.

"Look what it says there, now," Org Smit said, spelling out the words of one of the telegrams on the wall. "'President Kruger visits Johannesburg stop Miners' procession throws bottles stop.' Now, is there anything *in* that? And what's the idea of all those 'stops'?"

"Why, I remember the time when the only news we *had* was the sort the drum-men got over their drums," Johnny Welman said. "And it made sense, that sort of news. I am not ashamed to say that I brought up a family of six sons and three daughters on nothing else *but* that sort of news. And it was useful news to know. I can still remember the day when the message came over the drums about the three tax-collectors that had got eaten by crocodiles when their canoe capsized in the Limpopo. I don't mean that we were *glad* to hear that three tax-collectors had been eaten by crocodiles – "

And we all laughed and said, no, of course not.

Then Org Smit started spelling out another telegraph message pinned on the wall.

"'Fanatic shoots at King of Spain,'" he read. "'King unharmed stop. This enrages crowd which flings fanatic in royal fish-pond stop.'"

"What's the good of news like that to white farmers living in the Bushveld?" we asked of each other.

And when the telegraph-operator came from behind the counter to pin up another little bit of news we told him straight out what we thought. It was just a waste of money, we said, bringing the telegraph all that way up to Nietverdiend.

The telegraphist looked us up and down for a few moments in silence.

"Yes, I think it was a waste," he said, finally.

Boom – boom – boom – boom – boom – *boom*. Getting louder, do you notice? The whole village down there must be pretty drunk by now. Of course, why we can hear it so clearly is because of the direction of the wind.

Anyway, there was that other time when I again went to Mosigo and I told him about the King of Spain. And Mosigo said to me that he did not think much of that kind of news, and that if that was the best the white man could do with his telegraph wires, then the white man still had a lot to learn. The telegraph people could come right down to his hut and learn. Even though he did not have a yellow rod – like they had shown him on the roof of the post office – to keep the lightning away, but only a piece of python skin, he said.

Although I did not myself have a high opinion of the telegraph, I was not altogether pleased that an old kaffir like Mosigo should speak lightly of an invention that came out of the white man's brain. And so I said that the telegraph was still quite a new thing and that it would no doubt improve in time. Perhaps how it would improve quite a lot would be if they sacked that young telegraph-operator at Nietverdiend for a start, I said.

That young telegraph-operator was too impertinent, I said.

Mosigo agreed that it would help. It was a very important thing, he said, that for such work you should have the right sort of person. And then Mosigo asked if I could not perhaps put in a word for him in Pretoria for the telegraph-operator's job. He would one day – soon, even – show me how good he really was. It was no good, he explained, having news told to you by a man who was not suited to that kind of work. And Mosigo spat contemptuously on the ground beside the drum. You could see, then, how much he resented the competition that the telegraph-operator at Nietverdiend was introducing. Much as he would resent the spectacular achievements of a rival drum-man, I suppose.

"Another thing that is important is having the right person to tell the news to," Mosigo went on. "And you must also consider well as to whom the news is about. Take that king, now, of whom you have told me, that you heard of at Nietverdiend through the telegraph. He is a great chief, that king, is he not?"

I said to Mosigo that I should imagine that he must be a great chief, the King of Spain. I couldn't know for sure, of course. You can't, really, with foreigners.

"Has he many herds of cattle and many wives hoeing in the bean-fields?" Mosigo asked. "Has he many huts and does he drink much beer and is his stomach very fat? Do you know him well, this great chief?"

I told Mosigo that I did not know the King of Spain to speak to, since I had never met him. But if I did meet him – if the King of Spain came to the Dwarsberge, say – I would go up to him and say I was Schalk Lourens and he would say he was the King of Spain, and we would shake hands and talk about the crops and the drought and the Government – and perhaps about the new telegraph, even. We would talk together like any two white men would talk, I said.

But Mosigo explained that that was not what he meant. "What is the good of hearing about a man," he asked, "unless you know who that man *is*? When the telegraph-operator told you about that big chief, he told it to the wrong man."

Mosigo fell to beating his drum again. Boom – boom – boom – *boom* – boom – *boom* it went. Just like that drum down there in the village. Sounds wild, in the night, doesn't it? And did you hear that other sound? That one there, that shrill sound? I expected something like it. Yes, that shrill sound is a police whistle.

Some time later I was again at Nietverdiend. On the wall of the post office there were some more messages that Org Smit spelt out for us. Org Smit was on his way to Zeerust by ox-wagon with a load of mealies.

"Fanatic fires at Shah of Persia" – Org Smit read – "stop Misses stop Infuriated crowd throws fanatic in royal horse-trough stop."

On the way back from Nietverdiend I again called round at Mosigo's hut. I started telling him about the message that Org Smit had read out, but Mosigo interrupted me. Boom – boom – boom – *boom*, Mosigo's drum was going. . . By the way, do you hear how loud those drums are beating in the village? And the police whistle has stopped. I mean, it stopped suddenly. I hope it isn't serious trouble. . .

"Baas Org Smit?" Mosigo said to me. "Baas Org Smit is dead. A wagon with mealies went over him."

I did not wait to hear more. I climbed back on to my mule-cart and drove away fast along the road I had come. When I was almost halfway back to Nietverdiend I could still hear Mosigo's drum throbbing.

I had travelled a good distance along the Zeerust road and it was late afternoon when I saw a wagon that I recognised as Org Smit's and that was loaded high with mealies. The wagon was proceeding slowly down the dusty road. I made haste to overtake it. I drew close enough to see the driver. He was sitting on the seat and brandishing his long whip. From the back I recognised the driver as Org Smit. When I was almost abreast of the wagon I shouted. In the moment of Org Smit's turning round on the seat his whip caught in one of the wheels.

When I saw Org Smit fall from the wagon, I turned my face away.

The Homecoming

Laughter (Oom Schalk Lourens said). Well, there's a queer thing for you, now, and something not so easy to understand. And the older you get, the more things you seem to find to laugh at. Take old Frans Els, for instance. I can still remember the way he laughed, that time at Zeerust, when we were coming around the church building and we saw one of the tents from the Nagmaal camping-ground being carried away by a sudden gust of wind.

"It must be the ouderling's tent," Frans Els called out. "Well, he never was any good at fixing the ground-pegs. Look, kêrels, there it goes right across the road." And he laughed so much that his beard, which was turning white in places, flapped about almost like that tent in the wind.

Shortly afterwards, what was left of the tent got caught round the wooden poles of somebody's veranda, and several adults and a lot of children came running out of the house, shouting. By that time Frans Els was standing bent almost double over a fence. The tears were streaming down his cheeks and he had difficulty in getting his breath. I don't think I ever saw a man laugh so much in my life.

I don't think I ever saw a man stop laughing as quickly, either, as what Frans Els did when some people from the camping-ground came up and spoke to him. They had to say it over twice before he could get the full purport of the message, which was to the effect that it was not the ouderling's tent at all that had got blown away, but his.

I suppose you could describe the way in which Frans Els carried on that day while he still thought that it was the ouderling's tent, as one kind of laughter. The fact is that there are more kinds of laughter than just that one sort, and it seems to me that this is the cause of a lot of regrettable awkwardness in the world.

Another thing I have noticed is that when a woman laughs it usually means a good deal of trouble for a man. Not at that very moment, maybe, but afterwards. And more especially when it is a musical sort of laugh.

There is still another kind of laughter that you have also come across in your time, I am sure. That is the way we laugh when there are a number of us together in the Indian store at Ramoutsa, and Hendrik Moolman tells a funny story that he has read in the *Goede Hoop*. What is so entertaining about his way of telling these stories is that Hendrik Moolman always forgets what the point is. Then when we ask, "But what's so funny about it?" he tries to make up another story as he goes along. And because he's so weak at that, it makes us laugh more than ever.

So when we talk about Hendrik Moolman's funny stories, it is not the stories themselves that we find amusing, but his lack of skill in telling them. But I suppose it's all the same to Hendrik Moolman. He joins heartily in our laughter and waves his crutch about. Sometimes he even gets so excited that you almost expect him to rise up out of his chair without help.

It all happened very long ago, the first part of this story of Hendrik Moolman and his wife Malie. And in those days, when they had just married, you would not, if the idea of laughter had come into your mind, have thought first of Hendrik Moolman telling jokes in the Indian store.

They were just of an age, the young Moolman couple, and they were both good to look at. And when they arrived back from Zeerust after the wedding, Hendrik made a stirring show of the way he lifted Malie from the mule-cart, to carry her across the threshold of the little farmhouse in which their future life was to be cast. Needless to say, that was many years before Hendrik Moolman was to acquire the nickname of Crippled Hendrik, as the result of a fall into a diamond claim when he was drunk. Some said that his fall was an accident. Others saw in the occurrence the hand of the Lord.

What I remember most vividly about Malie, as she was in those early days of her marriage, were her eyes, and her laughter that was in such strange contrast to her eyes. Her laughter was free and clear and ringing. Each time you heard it, it was like a sudden bright light. Her laughter was like a summer's morning. But her eyes were dark and did not seem to belong with any part of the day at all.

It was the women who by and by started to say about the marriage of Hendrik and Malie this thing, that Malie's love for Hendrik was greater than his love for her. You could see it all, they said, by that look that came on her face when Hendrik entered the voorkamer, called in from the lands because there were visitors. You could tell it too, they declared, by that unnatural stillness that would possess her when she was left alone on the farm for a few days, as would happen each time her husband went with cattle or mealies to the market town.

With the years, also, that gay laugh of Malie Moolman's was heard more seldom, until in the end she seemed to have forgotten how to laugh at all. But there was never any suggestion of Malie having been unhappy. That was the queerest part of it – that part of the marriage of Malie and Hendrik that confuted all the busybodies. For it proved that Malie's devotion to Hendrik had not been just one-sided.

They had been married a good many years before that day when it became known to Malie – as a good while before that it had become known to the rest of the white people living on this side of the Dwarsberge – that Hendrik's return from the market town of Zeerust would be indefinitely delayed.

Those were prosperous times, and it was said that Hendrik had taken a considerable sum with him in gold coins for his journey to the Elandsputte diamond diggings, whither he had gone in the company of the Woman of Zeerust. Malie went on staying on the farm, and saw to it that the day-to-day activities in the kraal and on the lands and in the homestead went on just as though Hendrik were still there. Instead of in the arms of the Woman of Zeerust.

This went on for a good while, with Hendrik Moolman throwing away, on the diggings, real gold after visionary diamonds.

There were many curious features about this thing that had happened with Hendrik Moolman. For instance, it was known that he had written to his wife quite a number of times. Jurie Steyn, who kept the post office at Drogedal, had taken the trouble on one occasion to deliver into Malie's hands personally a letter addressed to her in her husband's handwriting. He had taken over the letter himself, instead of waiting for Malie to send for it. And Jurie Steyn said that Malie had thanked him very warmly for the letter, and had torn open the envelope in a state of agitation, and had wept over the contents of the letter, and had then informed Jurie Steyn that it was from her sister in Kuruman, who wrote about the drought there.

"It seemed to be a pretty long drought," Jurie Steyn said to us afterwards in the post office, "judging from the number of pages."

It was known, however, that when a woman visitor had made open reference to the state of affairs on the Elandsputte diggings, Malie had said that her husband was suffering from a temporary infatuation for the Woman of Zeerust, of whom she spoke without bitterness. Malie said she was certain that Hendrik would grow tired of that woman, and return to her.

Meanwhile, many rumours of what was happening with Hendrik Moolman on the Elandsputte diggings were conveyed to this part of the Marico by one means and another – mainly by donkey-cart. Later on it became known that Hendrik had sold the wagon and the oxen with which he had trekked from his farm to the diggings. Still later it became known why Malie was sending so many head of cattle to market. Finally, when a man with a waxed moustache and a notebook appeared in the neighbourhood, the farmers hereabouts, betokening no surprise, were able to direct him to the Moolman farm, where he went to take an inventory of the stock.

By that time the Woman of Zeerust must have discovered that Hendrik Moolman was about at the end of his resources. But nobody knew for sure when she deserted him – whether it was before or after that thing had happened to him which paralysed the left side of his body.

And that was how it came about that in the end Hendrik Moolman did return to his wife, Malie, just as she had during all that time maintained that he would. In reply to a message from Elandsputte diggings she had sent a kaffir in the mule-cart to fetch Baas Hendrik Moolman back to his farm.

Hendrik Moolman was seated in a half-reclining posture against the kaffir who held the reins, that evening when the mule-cart drew up in front of the home into which, many years before, on the day of their wedding, he had carried his wife, Malie. There was something not unfitting about his own homecoming in the evening, in the thought that Malie would be helping to lift him off the mule-cart, now.

Some such thought must have been uppermost in Malie's mind also. At all events, she came forward to greet her errant husband. Apparently she now comprehended for the first time the true extent of his incapacitation. Malie had not laughed for many years. Now the sound of her laughter, gay and silvery, sent its infectious echoes ringing through the farmyard.

Susannah and the Play-actor

I see a company of professional actors is going to stage a performance in the schoolroom at Drogedal (Oom Schalk Lourens said). There is a poster about it nailed to a kremetart tree in front of the building. I wonder what Henri le Valois thinks of it. His name is actually Hendrik de Waal, of course. But we still call him Le Valois in the Marico. And I wonder what his wife, Susannah, thinks of it also.

It's many years now since Henri le Valois quit the stage to go to work on his father-in-law's farm. But there seem to be more play-actors about than ever. The Agricultural Department has got rid of the worst of the locust plagues in these parts. But I suppose it will take more than Cooper's dip to thin out the professional actors.

The play presented by Henri le Valois in Zeerust – where I saw him on the stage for the first and last time – was about men who wore hats with ostrich-feathers and carried swords and had blankets slung over their shoulders, not striped, like the Basuto's, but black; and about women who had their hair put high up and wore jewels on their silk dresses but all the same did not look as grand as the men. Henri le Valois played the role of a young captain who falls in love with the king's wife and then leaves her in the end because of his loyalty to the king.

Henri le Valois was very fine in that last farewell scene. From my seat near the back of the hall I very much admired the way he walked out backwards, with his arms extended towards the queen, and saying, I must away adieu adieu for ever. Only a great actor, I felt, could walk out backwards like that and not trip over his sword or get the lower part of the blanket mixed up with his spurs.

The girls all fell in love with Henri le Valois, of course. Among them was Susannah Bekker, daughter of Petrus Bekker of Drogedal.

I wondered whether the girls would still feel attracted to him in the same way if they could have met him off-stage. I started wondering like that when I came across Henri le Valois in the bar of the Transvaal Hotel, one evening after the show, and most of the paint was washed off his face, and he was dressed just like me or At Naudé when we go into town and wear our shop clothes.

I hardly ever enter a bar, of course. I just happened to drop in on that evening because I thought I might find At Naudé there, and I wanted to talk to him about fetching some milk-cans for me from Ramoutsa. Strangely enough, At Naudé said that he had just dropped in on the off-chance of finding *me* there. And because this was such a peculiar coincidence, we thought it would be a good idea to reflect further on it over a glass of brandy. There were more coincidences like that as the evening wore on and other farmers from the Groot Marico came into the bar, also just on the off-chance.

When the coincidences had reached the stage where the bar was so full of farmers that you couldn't walk – then it was that Henri le Valois came in. He was accompanied by Alwyn Klopper who acted the part of the king in the play.

But before the arrival in the bar of these two actors, a great deal of talk had been going on about them. Somebody mentioned that Henri le Valois's real name was Hendrik de Waal, and that he had taken that foreign-sounding name so that he could move about better on the stage. The name helped him particularly in the showy farewell scene at the end, that person added. You couldn't believe then that he was actually just an ordinary farmer's son, who had once herded cattle over rough veld with polgras, when you saw how gracefully he went off the stage – as though he was pedalling a push-bike backwards. We also said that it was quite clear why Alwyn Klopper didn't also change his name to something French. The size of his feet were against him.

Henri le Valois seemed surprised to find the bar so crowded when he came in, accompanied by the king. He explained that his play-acting company was concerned with improving the minds of the people living in the backveld and with bringing culture to the Boers, and so he naturally did not frequent tap rooms. He had only dropped in there for some purpose which he had forgotten now. It had gone clean out of his mind, he said, through the shock of finding so many members of his audience in a public bar. He drank a couple of quick double brandies to get over the shock.

When it was explained to him that most of the farmers in that bar room were not members of his audience, or likely to be, he seemed to feel better about it, at first. Afterwards he didn't seem so sure.

A little later, when he had had a few more double brandies, Henri le Valois, standing against the crowded counter with a cigarette in the side of his mouth, gave us an interesting talk on what he referred to as the higher ideals of his art.

"Why, do you know," he said, "tonight I counted no less than nine people in the half-crown seats."

He had put on the play about himself and the king in every dorp from Zwartruggens to Zeerust, he said, and it had everywhere been a great cultural success. The biggest cultural success had been at Rysmierbult, where he had cleared over eleven pounds, after paying for the hall and the hotel bills of the touring company.

"Strictly speaking, Slurry was still more of a cultural success," he added. "I mean, we left Slurry with even more money. Only, we had a little misunderstanding with the hotel proprietor, who kept a couple of suitcases behind. Fortunately, they were suitcases belonging to the minor members of our company and whom we could replace. Yes, you have no idea how much we artists have to suffer."

Henri le Valois grew more and more sad. He turned to Alwyn Klopper, the king, who during all this time had been standing next to him, silent and not drinking much.

"That pigskin suitcase with the gold monogram, who did it belong to?" Henri le Valois asked him.

"To a school-teacher at Krugersdorp," the king answered, shortly. "But don't worry about her. She got a lift back home on a lorry."

"And that black-and-white portmanteau with the wavy initials – " Le Valois began again. By this time he was so sad that if he hadn't held tight on to the edge of the counter he would have fallen.

"Wolmaransstad," the king snapped. "He was a former income-tax official. Nobody would give *him* a lift back home."

So Henri le Valois went on drinking large quantities of brandy. In the end he was crying into his glass. And all the time the king stood watching him, smiling and drinking scarcely at all.

Suddenly Henri le Valois thrust the glass away from him and drew himself up to look very tall and imposing.

"All those beautiful suitcases," he cried.

Then he stood back a couple of paces from the king.

"I quit," he said to Alwyn Klopper. "You take over. I shall not be unfaithful further. Farewell I must away adieu adieu for ever."

And he started back-pedalling out of the bar.

There were those present in the bar that night who said of Henri le Valois that he had never acted more grandly, more magnificently, in his life than in that scene in which he took final leave of the stage. I also thought that it was most impressive, the way he made his way out through the curtains at the bar entrance, turning his feet half outwards, as though he still had spurs on them, and making a wide sweep with his left arm as though from his waist there hung a sword.

When he bared his hat in a farewell bow, I could almost have believed that there was a painted ostrich plume decorating his grey felt hat.

And that was the moment in which Susannah Bekker, passing the hotel on her way back to the boarding-house where she was staying for the Nagmaal week with her parents, encountered Henri le Valois. She had before seen him only on the stage, dressed as a gallant. And so she recognised him immediately, then, in front of the bar, not from his clothing but from his bearing. They got talking, Susannah told me about it long afterwards, and she was thrilled by how human he was. This was a greater thrill than anything she had felt about him when she had seen him on the stage, even. Especially when he talked about how he was being bullied all the time by the king, who had no soul and no feelings.

"I realised that Henri le Valois was not only a very fine human being," Susannah said, finally, "but also a very great actor. He was play-acting drunk. What do you think of that?"

There was no call for me to tell her that that part of it hadn't been play-acting.

Sold Down the River

We had, of course, heard of André Maritz's play and his company of play-actors long before they got to Zeerust (Oom Schalk Lourens said).

For they had travelled a long road. Some of the distance they went by train. Other parts of the way they travelled by mule-cart or ox-wagon. They visited all the dorps from the Cape – where they had started from – to Zeerust in the Transvaal, where Hannekie Roodt left the company. She had an important part in the play, as we knew even before we saw her name in big letters on the posters.

André Maritz had been somewhat thoughtless, that time, in his choice of a play for his company to act in. The result was that there were some places that he had to go away from at a pace rather faster than could be made by even a good mule-team. Naturally, this sort of thing led to André Maritz's name getting pretty well known throughout the country – and without his having to stick up posters, either.

The trouble did not lie with the acting. There was not very much wrong with that. But anybody could have told André Maritz that he should never have toured the country with that kind of a play. There was a negro in it, called Uncle Tom, who was supposed to be very good and kind-hearted. André Maritz, with his face blackened, took that part. And there was also a white man in the play, named Simon Legree. He was the kind of white man who, if he was your neighbour, would think it funny to lead the Government tax-collector to the aarvark-hole that you were hiding in.

It seems that André Maritz had come across a play that had been popular on the other side of the sea; and he translated it into Afrikaans and adapted it to fit in with South African traditions. André Maritz's fault was that he hadn't adapted the play enough.

The company made this discovery in the very first Free State dorp they got to. For, when they left that town, André Maritz had one of his eyes blackened, and not just with burnt cork.

André Maritz adapted his play a good deal more, immediately after that. He made Uncle Tom into a much less kind-hearted negro. And he also made him steal chickens.

The only member of the company that the public of the backveld seemed to have any time for was the young man who acted Simon Legree.

Thus it came about that we heard of André Maritz's company when they were still far away, touring the highveld. Winding their play-actors' road northwards, past koppies and through vlaktes, and by bluegums and willows.

After a few more misunderstandings with the public, André Maritz so far adapted the play to South African conditions as to make Uncle Tom threaten to hit Topsy with a brandy bottle.

The result was that, by the time the company came to Zeerust, even the church elder, Theunis van Zyl, said that there was much in the story of Uncle Tom that could be considered instructive.

True, there were still one or two little things, Elder van Zyl declared, that did not perhaps altogether accord with what was best in our outlook. For instance, it was not right that we should be made to feel so sentimental about the slave-girl as played by Hannekie Roodt. The elder was referring to that powerful scene in which Hannekie Roodt got sold down the river by Simon Legree. We couldn't understand very clearly what it meant to be sold down the river. But from Hannekie Roodt's acting we could see that it must be the most awful fate that could overtake anybody.

She was so quiet. She did not speak in that scene. She just picked up the small bundle containing her belongings. Then she put her hand up to her coat collar and closed over the lapel in front, even though the weather was not cold.

Yet there were still some people in Zeerust who, after they had attended the play on the first night, thought that that scene could be improved on. They said that when Hannekie Roodt walked off the stage for the last time, sold down the river, and carrying the bundle of her poor possessions tied up in a red-spotted rag, a few of her mistress's knives and forks could have been made to drop out of the bundle.

As I have said, André Maritz's company eventually arrived in Zeerust. They came by mule-cart from Slurry, where the railway ended in those days. They stayed at the Marico Hotel, which was a few doors from Elder van Zyl's house. It was thus that André Maritz met Deborah, the daughter of the elder. That was one thing that occasioned a good deal of talk. Especially as we believed that even if Hannekie Roodt was not actually married to André Maritz in the eyes of the law, the two of them were nevertheless as nearly husband and wife as it is possible for play-actors to be, since they are known to be very unenlightened in such matters.

The other things that gave rise to much talk had to do with what happened on the first night of the staging of the play in Zeerust. André Maritz hired the old hall adjoining the mill. The hall had last been used two years before.

The result was that, after the curtain had gone up for the first act of André Maritz's play, it was discovered that a wooden platform above the stage was piled high with fine flour that had sifted through the ceiling from the mill next door. The platform had been erected by the stage company that had given a performance in the hall two years previously. That other company had used the platform to throw down bits of paper from to look like snow, in a scene in which a girl gets thrust out into the world with her baby in her arms.

At the end of the first act, when the curtain was lowered, André Maritz had the platform swept. But until then, with all that flour coming down, it looked as though he and his company were moving about the stage in a Cape mist. Each time an actor took a step forward or spoke too loudly – down would come a shower of fine meal. Afterwards the players took to standing in one place as much as possible, to avoid shaking down the flour – and in fear of losing their way in the mist, too, by the look of things.

Naturally, all this confused the audience a good deal. For, with the flour sifting down on to the faces of the actors, it became difficult, after a little while, to tell which were the white people and which the negroes. Towards the end of the first act Uncle Tom, with a layer of flour covering his make-up, looked just as white as Simon Legree.

During the time when the curtain was lowered, however, the flour was swept from the platform and the actors repaired their faces very neatly, so that when the next act began there was nothing anymore to remind us of that first unhappy incident.

Later on I was to think that it was a pity that the consequences of that *second* unhappy incident, that of André Maritz's meeting with the daughter of Elder van Zyl, could not also have been brushed away so tidily.

The play was nevertheless very successful. And I am sure that in the crowded hall that night there were very few dry eyes when Hannekie Roodt played her great farewell scene. When she picked up her bundle and got ready to leave, having been sold down the river, you could see by her stillness that her parting from her lover and her people would be for ever. No one who saw her act that night would ever forget the tragic moment when she put her hand up to her coat collar and closed over the lapels in front, even though – as I have said – the weather was not cold.

The applause at the end lasted for many minutes.

The play got the same enthusiastic reception night after night. Meanwhile, off the stage, there were many stories linking Deborah van Zyl's name with André Maritz's.

"They say that Deborah van Zyl is going to be an actress now," Flip Welman said when several of us were standing smoking in the hardware store. "She is supposed to be getting Hannekie Roodt's part."

"We all know that Deborah van Zyl has been talking for a long while about going on the stage," Koos Steyn said. "And maybe this is the chance she was been waiting for. But I can't see her in Hannekie Roodt's part for very long. I think she will rather be like the girl in that other play we saw here a few years ago – the one with the baby."

Knowing what play-actors were, I could readily picture Deborah van Zyl being pushed out into the world, carrying a child in her arms, and with the white-paper snow fluttering about her.

As for Hannekie Roodt, she shortly afterwards left André Maritz's company of play-actors. She arranged with Koos Steyn to drive her, with her suitcases, to Slurry station. Koos explained to me that he was a married man and so he could not allow it to be said of him, afterwards, that he had driven alone in a cart with a play-actress. That was how it came about that I rode with them.

But Koos Steyn need have had no fears of the kind that he hinted at. Hannekie Roodt spoke hardly a word. At close hand she looked different from what she had done on the stage. Her hair was scraggy. I also noticed that her teeth were uneven and that there was loose skin at her throat.

Yet, there was something about her looks that was not without a strange sort of beauty. And in her presence there was that which made me think of great cities. There were also marks on her face from which you could tell that she had travelled a long road. A road that was longer than just the thousand miles from the Cape to the Marico.

Hannekie Roodt was going away from André Maritz. And during the whole of that long journey by mule-cart she did not once weep. I could not help but think that it was true what people said about play-actors. They had no real human feelings. They could act on the stage and bring tears to your eyes, but they themselves had no emotions.

We arrived at Slurry station. Hannekie Roodt thanked Koos Steyn and paid him. There was no platform there in those days. So Hannekie had to climb up several steps to get on to the balcony of the carriage. It was almost as though she were getting on to the stage. We lifted up her suitcases for her.

Koos Steyn and I returned to the mule-cart. Something made me look back over my shoulder. That was my last glimpse of Hannekie Roodt. I saw her put her hand up to her coat collar. She closed over the lapels in front. The weather was not cold.

Tryst by the Vaal

"Three is no company."

It was the landdrost's man who spoke these words (Oom Schalk Lourens said). The landdrost's man made that comment when three people kept a tryst by the willows on the Vaal.

I was on my way to the town with a load of mealies, that time when the Vaal was in flood. It was not a big load, because of the stalk-borer. A short distance away Nicolaas Vermeulen was standing with his trek. His wagon had been outspanned there for several days. He, too, had been making his way to the dorp and had been held up by floodwaters. Nicolaas Vermeulen was on a visit to relatives and had brought his wife and family with him. Along with his family, Nicolaas Vermeulen had with him, on his wagon, Miemie Retief, who was about nineteen years of age. Miemie Retief was the daughter of a neighbour. She was supposed to be accompanying the Vermeulens to town also in order to visit relatives.

Still further away Gerrit Huyser was camped. He had arrived at the drift a little while before Nicolaas Vermeulen. He had a kaffir to help with the oxen. But otherwise he was travelling alone. Gerrit Huyser's farm was some distance further up along the Vaal River.

He was now camped on the same outspan with Nicolaas Vermeulen and myself, but had drawn his wagon up nearer the drift, so that when the river went down he would be the first to cross.

I learnt from Nicolaas Vermeulen and his wife that Gerrit Huyser was on his way to the diamond diggings. Well, the mealie crop had been a failure in most parts of the Transvaal that year, and Gerrit Huyser was not the only farmer from that area who had decided to try his luck on the diggings for a while. And because of what had happened with the mealies, I suppose that more than one farmer, in turning up a diamond on the sorting table, would first look to see if there wasn't a stalk-borer in it.

What was singular about Gerrit Huyser's trek, however, was the kind of load he had on his wagon. It looked to be mostly household furniture. We could see that from where the bucksails did not fit properly.

One evening Nicolaas Vermeulen and his wife and I sat in front of their family tent after supper, drinking coffee.

Nicolaas Vermeulen's children played around the camp-fire while we talked and Miemie Retief, the daughter of their neighbour, sat on a riempies stool some distance from us. She had threaded a red ribbon into her black hair. And I was glad of it. Here on a lonely part of the veld, next to a river in flood, where there was nobody to see her – as you would think – she still wanted to appear at her best.

I regretted that I hadn't thought of wearing my new veldskoens.

After Nicolaas Vermeulen and I had, each in turn, said that it would probably take another two days for the river to go down enough for us to be able to cross, the conversation turned to Gerrit Huyser.

"It's not as though he has sold up," Nicolaas Vermeulen said, "and no farmer goes and stays on the diggings for more than a few months. When I first saw his wagon loaded up so high I thought it was with tree-trunks that he had fished out of the flooded river. I thought it was firewood – "

"If he's brought along that big tamboetie-wood cupboard in which his wife keeps those plates with the blue twigs painted on them," Nicolaas Vermeulen's wife, Martha, interrupted him, "then it might perhaps not be so foolish, after all. That's about all that cupboard is any good for – to light the fire with. . . The airs she gives herself over that piece of junk."

I mentioned that I had that very morning also seen Gerrit Huyser's rusbank on the wagon. I had seen it while I was talking to Gerrit Huyser, I explained, and a gust of wind had raised a corner of the wagon-sail. Later in the day I had seen him fasten down that flap with an ox-riem.

So we said that it looked as though Gerrit Huyser intended taking things in rather too easy a way on the diggings.

"I suppose he thinks he can sit back on that rusbank and watch the kaffirs work," Nicolaas Vermeulen said. "Just as though he's still at home on his farm."

We said that with all that furniture in his tent on the diggings, it looked as though Gerrit Huyser was expecting company. We started to wonder if he would have the coloured portrait of the president hanging on the inside of his tent, opposite his family tree in its gold frame – just like in his voorkamer at home.

It was then that Martha Vermeulen asked what Gerrit Huyser's wife would be doing all that time on the farm, alone and without any furniture in the house.

"Anyway," I said, "she'll find it easy to keep the place tidy."

I said this several times. But Nicolaas Vermeulen and his wife did not laugh. I looked quickly in the direction of Miemie Retief. The light from the fire made pictures on her cheeks and forehead.

That was the moment when Gerrit Huyser arrived in our midst. He came out of the veld, where a dark wind was, and he moved slowly and ponderously. For a moment he stood between us and the fire, his shoulders high against the night. Then he took off his hat in a way that seemed to hold in it a kind of challenge.

Nicolaas Vermeulen invited him to sit down. Gerrit Huyser found a place for himself that was furthest away from where Miemie Retief was seated.

We spoke first in general terms, and then I mentioned to Gerrit Huyser that he would find quite a number of farmers from our area on the diggings. There were Stoffel Lange and his cousin Maans and Oupa Snyman and almost all the Bekkers, not even to mention the farmers from the Kromberg section.

"Anyway, if they all come to visit you at the same time in your tent on the diggings," Nicolaas Vermeulen said, playfully, "you'll have chairs for them all."

I was surprised at the way Nicolaas Vermeulen was talking.

"And if you find a big diamond you'll be able to buy yourself a new span of red Afrikaner oxen, with their coats all shining," Nicolaas Vermeulen chuckled. "And you'll be able to get perhaps even a new wife."

I looked down at the ground and felt uncomfortable. When I glanced up again I could see that Martha Vermeulen had nudged her husband. She had nudged him almost off the upturned candle-box he was sitting on. The Vermeulens, at all events – I realised – had not brought many chairs with them.

I suddenly thought of looking at Miemie Retief. She was sitting with her head bent slightly forward and with her eyes cast on the ground, as mine had been. Then she raised her head again, and in the swift look that passed between herself and Gerrit Huyser I understood that it would have made no difference if I had thought of wearing my new veldskoens that evening.

The little party in front of the Vermeulens' tent broke up shortly afterwards.

But the things Nicolaas Vermeulen had to tell me next morning did not come as a surprise to me. He told me of Miemie Retief's meeting with Gerrit Huyser under the stars. He said that his wife, Martha, had watched those two from behind the flap of the tent.

"Miemie's coming with my wife and me was just a trick of hers to get away from home," Nicolaas Vermeulen said. "It is clear that she and Gerrit Huyser had an appointment to meet here by the Vaal. How it will all end, the good Lord only knows."

You can imagine for yourself the strain that was in the situation after that. When we were all five of us together, we spoke nervously about unimportant things. When I was with Nicolaas Vermeulen and his wife we spoke of Miemie Retief and Gerrit Huyser. But what Miemie Retief and Gerrit Huyser spoke about at those times when they were alone together, I suppose no one can tell.

Hour after hour we waited for the river to go down. But nobody scanned the floodwaters more anxiously than did Gerrit Huyser.

Nicolaas Vermeulen's wife said she was convinced that Gerrit Huyser would yet murder us all in our sleep. She was also sure that he had murdered his wife and had brought her along on the wagon, lying in that tall cupboard. Every murder story had a chest or something like that in it, for the body.

"And how she used to polish that cupboard with olieblaar," Martha Vermeulen added. "I can't bear to think of it. The poor thing – lying there, in amongst those plates with all the blue twigs painted on them."

I tried to comfort her by saying that Gerrit Huyser would at least have had the forethought to take the plates out first.

Martha Vermeulen's agitation had an unhappy effect on both Nicolaas and myself.

Meanwhile, it seemed to me that Gerrit Huyser's wagon wore a doomed look, somehow, with all that furniture piled on it. And it was at the wagon that Gerrit Huyser and Miemie Retief were standing when two men called on Gerrit Huyser. Even at a distance we could tell, from their official air, that the visitors were landdrost's men. Gerrit did not take some chairs down from the wagon for his guests to sit on.

And, as always seems to happen in such cases, it was at about that time, also, that the third person in this affair arrived. She came there, to the trysting place, under the willows by the Vaal, where wild birds sang.

The landdrost's men lifted her out of the water and loosened the oxriems that had bound her feet over the long distance that the flooded river had carried her. And it was after they had laid the body of Gerrit Huyser's wife in the tall tamboetie cupboard that one of the landdrost's men made the remark that, earlier on, I told you of. – "Three," the landdrost's man said, "is no company."

The Lover Who Came Back

It caused no small stir in the Marico (Oom Schalk Lourens said) when Piet Human came back after an absence of twenty years. His return was as unexpected as his departure had been sudden.

It was quite a story, the manner of his leaving the farm his father had bought for him at Gemsbokvlei, and also the reasons for his leaving. Since it was a story of young love, the women took pleasure in discussing it in much detail.

The result was that with the years the events surrounding Piet Human's sudden decision to move out of the Marico remained fresh in people's memories. More, the affair grew into something like a folk-tale, almost, with the passage of time.

Indeed, I heard one version of the story of Piet Human and the girl Wanda Rossouw as far away as Schweizer-Reneke, where I had trekked with my cattle during a season of drought. It was told me by one of the daughters in the house of a farmer with whom I had made arrangements for grazing my cattle.

The main feature of the story was the wooden stile between the two farms – Piet Human's farm and the farm of Wanda Rossouw's parents. If you brought that stile into it, you could not go wrong in the telling of the story, whatever else you added to it or left out.

And so the farmer's daughter in Schweizer-Reneke, because she mentioned the stile at the beginning, related the story very pleasantly.

Piet Human had been courting Wanda Rossouw for some time. And they had met often by the white-painted wooden fence that stood at the boundary of the two farms. And Wanda Rossouw had dark eyes and a wild heart.

Now, it had been well known that, before Piet Human came to live at Gemsbokvlei, there had been another young man who had called very regularly at the Rossouw homestead. This young man was Gerhard Oelofse. He was somewhat of a braggart. But he had dashing ways. In his stride there was a kind of freedom that you could not help noticing. It was said that there were few girls in the Groot Marico that Gerhard Oelofse could not have for the asking.

One day Gerhard Oelofse rode off to join Van Pittius's freebooters in Stellaland. Later on he left for the Caprivi Strip. From then onwards we would receive, at long intervals, vague accounts of his activities in those distant parts. And in those fragmentary items of news about Gerhard Oelofse that reached us, there was little that did him credit.

Anyway, to return to Wanda Rossouw and Piet Human. There was an afternoon near to the twilight when they again met at the stile on the boundary between the two farms. It was a low stile, with only two crosspieces. And the moment came inevitably when Piet Human, standing on his side of the fence, stooped forward to take Wanda Rossouw in his arms and lift her over to him. And in that moment Wanda Rossouw told him of what had happened, two years before, between Gerhard Oelofse and herself.

Piet Human had Wanda Rossouw in his arms. He put her down again, awkwardly, on her own side of the fence; and without a word walked away from her, into the deepening twilight.

Soon afterwards he sold his farm and left the Marico.

Because of the prominence she gave to that wooden stile, the daughter of the farmer in Schweizer-Reneke told the story of Piet Human and Wanda Rossouw remarkably well. True, she introduced into her narrative a few variations that were unfamiliar to us in the Groot Marico, but that made no difference to the quality of the story itself.

When she came to the end of the tale, I mentioned to her that I actually knew that wooden fence – low, with two cross-rails, and painted white. I had seen that stile very often, I said.

The farmer's daughter looked at me with a new sort of interest. She looked at me in such a way that for a little while I felt almost as though I was handsome. On the spur of the moment I went so far as to make up a lie. I told her that I had even carved my initials on that stile. On one of the lower cross-rails, I said. I felt it would have been too presumptuous if I had said one of the upper rails.

But even as I spoke I realised, by the far-off look in her eyes, that the farmer's daughter had already lost interest in me.

Ah, well, the story of Piet Human and Wanda Rossouw was a good love story and I had no right to try to chop a piece of it out for myself, cutting – in imagination – 'Schalk Lourens' into a strip of painted wood with a pocket knife.

"If Piet Human had really loved Wanda Rossouw, he would have forgiven her for what had happened with Gerhard Oelofse," the daughter of the Schweizer-Reneke farmer said, dreamily. "At least, I think so. But I suppose you can never tell. . . "

And so, when Piet Human came back to the Marico, the story of his sudden departure, twenty years earlier, was still fresh in people's memories – and with sundry additions.

I heard of Piet Human's return several weeks before I met him. Indeed, everyone north of the Dwarsberge knew he had come back. We talked of nothing else.

Where I again met him, after twenty years, was in Jurie Bekker's post office. He was staying with Jurie Bekker. I must admit that there were some unhappy aspects of that meeting for me; and I have reason to believe that there were those of the older farmers in Jurie Bekker's post office that day – men who had also known Piet Human long before – who felt as I did. For when Piet Human left us he was a young man of five-and-twenty summers. We saw him again now as a man of mature years. There were wrinkles under his eyes, there were grey hairs at his temples and – with our sudden awareness that Piet Human had indeed grown twenty years older since we had seen him came the knowledge that we, too, each of us, had also aged.

How I knew that others felt as I did was that, when I glanced across at Jurie Bekker, he was sitting back in his chair with his eyes cast down to his stomach. He gazed at his fat stomach with a certain intentness for some moments, and then shook his head sadly.

But it did not last long, this sense of melancholy. We soon shook from our spirits the first stirrings of gloom. Those intervening years that the locusts had eaten were no more than a quick sigh. We drank our coffee and listened to what Piet Human had to tell and in a little while it was as though he had never gone away.

Piet Human told us that he had entered the Marico from the Bechuanaland side and had journeyed through Ramoutsa. He had decided to stay with Jurie Bekker for a time and had not yet, in his visits to familiar scenes of twenty years before, gone farther to the west along the Government Road.

I thought this statement of Piet Human's significant. Farther to the west lay the farm that had once been his, Gemsbokvlei; and adjoining it was the Rossouw farm, where Wanda Rossouw still lived with her widowed mother. For all those years Wanda Rossouw, though attractive and sought after, had remained unmarried.

Piet Human said that in some ways the Marico had changed a great deal since he had been there last. In other respects there had been no changes at all. Some of the people he had known had died; others had trekked away. And children in arms had grown into young men and women.

But there were just as many features of life in the Marico that had not changed.

"I came here through Rooigrond," Piet Human said. "That big white house that used to be the headquarters of the Van Pittius freebooter gang is still there. But it is today a coach station."

He had asked how much he would have to pay for a coach ticket to Ottoshoop, and when they told him, he realised that the place had not changed at all; that big white house was still the headquarters of robbers.

Then there were those Mtosa huts on the way to Ramoutsa.

Thus Piet Human entertained us. But I noticed that all his stories related only to places on the Ramoutsa side of the Marico. He made no reference to that other side where his old farm was, and where the Rossouws dwelt.

We were naturally very curious to know what his plans were, but there was nobody in the post office that afternoon so coarse-grained as even to hint at the past. We all felt that the story of Piet Human and Wanda Rossouw stood for something in our community; there was a fineness about it that we meant to respect.

Even Fritz van Tonder, who was known as a pretty rough character, waited until Piet Human had gone out of the voorkamer before he said anything. And all he said then was, "Well, if Piet Human has decided to forgive Wanda Rossouw for that Gerhard Oelofse business he'll find she's still pretty. And she has waited long enough."

We ignored his remarks.

But the day did come when Piet Human paid a visit to that other part of the Marico where his old farm was. The white-painted wooden stile stood there still. The uprights, before being put into the ground, had been dipped in a Stockholm tar of a kind that you do not get today. And it was when the twilight was beginning to fall that Piet Human again saw Wanda Rossouw by the stile. She wore a pale frock. And although her face had perhaps grown thinner with the years, the look in her dark eyes had not changed. The grass was heavy with the scents of a dying summer's day.

Piet Human spoke urgent, burning words in a low voice. He leaned forward over the fence and took Wanda Rossouw in his arms.

She struggled in his arms, thrusting him from her fiercely when he tried to lift her over the stile.

Then at last Piet Human understood – that it was that other, worthless lover, who had forgotten her years ago, for whom, down the years, vainly, Wanda Rossouw waited.

For the second time Piet Human walked into the gathering dusk alone.

The Selon's Rose

Any story (Oom Schalk Lourens said) about that half-red flower, the selon's rose, must be an old story. It is the flower that a Marico girl most often pins in her hair to attract a lover. The selon's rose is also the flower that here, in the Marico, we customarily plant upon a grave.

One thing that certain thoughtless people sometimes hint at about my stories is that nothing ever seems to happen in them. Then there is another kind of person who goes even further, and *he* says that the stories I tell are all stories that he has heard before, somewhere, long ago – he can't remember when, exactly, but somewhere at the back of his mind he knows that it is not a new story.

I have heard that remark passed quite often – which is not surprising, seeing that I really don't know any new stories. But the funny part of it is that these very people will come around, say, ten years later, and ask me to tell them another story. And they will say, then, because of what they have learnt of life in between, that the older the better.

Anyway, I have come to the conclusion that with an old story it is like with an old song. People tire of a new song readily. I remember how it was when Marie Dupreez came back to the Bushveld after her parents had sent her overseas to learn singing, because they had found diamonds on their farm, and because Marie's teacher said she had a nice singing voice. Then, when Marie came back from Europe – through the diamonds on the Dupreez farm having given out suddenly – we on this side of the Dwarsberge were keen to have Marie sing for us.

There was a large attendance, that night, when Marie Dupreez gave a concert in the Drogedal schoolroom. She sang what she called arias from Italian opera. And at first things didn't go at all well. We didn't care much for those new songs in Italian. One song was about the dawn being near, goodbye beloved and about being under somebody's window – that was what Marie's mother told us it was.

Marie Dupreez's mother came from the Cape and had studied at the Wellington seminary. Another song was about mother see these tears. The Hollander schoolmaster told me the meaning of that one. But I didn't know if it was Marie's mother that was meant.

We didn't actually dislike those songs that Marie Dupreez sang. It was only that we weren't moved by them.

Accordingly, after the interval, when Marie was again stepping up on to the low platform before the blackboard on which the teacher wrote sums on school days, Philippus Bonthuys, a farmer who had come all the way from Nietverdiend to attend the concert, got up and stood beside Marie Dupreez. And because he was so tall and broad it seemed almost as though he stood half in front of her, elbowing her a little, even.

Philippus Bonthuys said that he was just a plain Dopper. And we all cheered. Then Philippus Bonthuys said that his grandfather was also just a plain Dopper, who wore his pipe and his tobacco-bag on a piece of string fastened at the side of his trousers. We cheered a lot more, then. Philippus Bonthuys went on to say that he liked the old songs best. They could keep those new songs about laugh because somebody has stolen your clown. We gathered from this that Marie's mother had been explaining to Philippus Bonthuys, also, in quick whispers, the meanings of some of Marie's songs.

And before we knew where we were, the whole crowd in the schoolroom was singing, with Philippus Bonthuys beating time, "My Oupa was 'n Dopper, en 'n Dopper was Hy." You've got no idea how stirring that old song sounded, with Philippus Bonthuys beating time, in the night, under the thatch of that Marico schoolroom, and with Marie Dupreez looking slightly bewildered but joining in all the same – since it was her concert, after all – and not singing in Italian, either.

We sang many songs, after that, and they were all old songs. We sang "Die Vaal Hare en die Blou Oge" and "Daar Waar die Son en die Maan Ondergaan" and "Vat Jou Goed en Trek, Ferreira" and "Met My Rooi Rok Voor Jou Deur." It was very beautiful.

We sang until late into the night. Afterwards, when we congratulated Marie Dupreez's mother, who had arranged it all, on the success of her daughter's concert, Mevrou Dupreez said it was nothing, and she smiled. But it was a peculiar sort of smile.

I felt that she must have smiled very much the same way when she was informed that the diamond mine on the Dupreez farm was only an alluvial gravel-bed, and not a pipe, like in Kimberley.

Now, Marie Dupreez had not been out of the Marico very long. All told, I don't suppose she had been in Europe for more than six months before the last shovelful of diamondiferous gravel went through Dupreez's sieve. By the time she got back, her father was so desperate that he was even trying to sift ordinary Transvaal red clay. But Marie's visit overseas had made her restive.

That, of course, is something that I can't understand. I have also been to foreign parts. During the Boer War I was a prisoner on St. Helena. And I was twice in Johannesburg. And one thing about St. Helena is that there were no Uitlanders on it. There were just Boers and English and Coloureds and Indians, like you come across here in the Marico. There were none of those all-sorts that you've got to push past on Johannesburg pavements. And each time I got back to my own farm, and I could sit on my stoep and fill my pipe with honest Magaliesberg tobacco, I was pleased to think I was away from all that sin that you read about in the Bible.

But with Marie Dupreez it was different.

Marie Dupreez, after she came back from Europe, spoke a great deal about how unhappy a person with a sensitive nature could be over certain aspects of life in the Marico.

We were not unwilling to agree with her.

"When I woke up that morning at Nietverdiend," Willie Prinsloo said to Marie during a party at the Dupreez homestead, "and I found that I couldn't inspan my oxen because during the night the Mlapi kaffirs had stolen my trek-chain – well, to a person with a sensitive nature, I can't tell you how unhappy I felt about the Marico."

Marie said that was the sort of thing that made her ill, almost.

"It's always the same kind of conversation that you have to listen to, day in and day out," Marie Dupreez said. "A farmer outspans his oxen for the night. And next morning, when he has to move on, the kaffirs have stolen his trek-chain. I don't know how often I have heard that same story. Why can't something different ever happen? Why can't a kaffir think of stealing something else, for a change?"

"Yes," Jurie Bekker interjected, quickly, "why can't they steal a clown, say?"

Thereupon Marie explained that it was not a clown that had got stolen in that Italian song that she sang in the schoolroom, but a girl who had belonged to a clown. And so several of us said, speaking at the same time, that she couldn't have been much of a girl, anyway, belonging to a clown. We said we might be behind the times and so forth, here in the Bushveld, but we had seen clowns in the circus in Zeerust, and we could imagine what a clown's girl must be like, with her nose painted all red.

I must admit, however, that we men enjoyed Marie's wild talk. We preferred it to her singing, anyway. And the women also listened quite indulgently.

Shortly afterwards Marie Dupreez made a remark that hurt me, a little.

"People here in the Marico say all the same things over and over again," Marie announced. "Nobody ever says anything new. You all talk just like the people in Oom Schalk Lourens's stories. Whenever we have visitors it's always the same thing. If it's a husband and wife, it will be the man who first starts talking. And he'll say that his Afrikaner cattle are in a bad way with the heart-water. Even though he drives his cattle straight out on to the veld with the first frost, and he keeps to regular seven-day dipping, he just can't get rid of the heart-water ticks."

Marie Dupreez paused. None of us said anything, at first. I only know that for myself I thought this much: I thought that, even though I dip my cattle only when the Government inspector from Onderstepoort is in the neighbourhood, I still lose just as many Afrikaner beasts from the heart-water as any of the farmers hereabouts who go in for the seven-day dipping.

"They should dip the Onderstepoort inspector every seven days," Jurie Bekker called out suddenly, expressing all our feelings.

"And they should drive the Onderstepoort inspector straight out on to the veld first with the first frost," Willie Prinsloo added.

We got pretty worked up, I can tell you.

"And it's the same with the women," Marie Dupreez went on. "Do they ever discuss books or fashion or music? No. They also talk just like those simple Boer women that Oom Schalk Lourens's head is so full of. They talk about the amount of Kalahari sand that the Indian in the store at Ramoutsa mixed with the last bag of yellow sugar they bought off him. You know, I have heard that same thing so often, I am surprised that there is any sand at all left in the Kalahari desert, the way that Indian uses it all up."

Those of us who were in the Dupreez voorkamer that evening, in spite of our amusement, also felt sad at the thought of how Marie Dupreez had altered from her natural self, like a seedling that has been transplanted too often in different kinds of soil.

But we felt that Marie should not be blamed too much. For one thing, her mother had been taught at that women's college at the Cape. And her father had also got his native knowledge of the soil pretty mixed up, in his own way. It was said that he was by now even trying to find diamonds in the turfgrond on his farm. I could just imagine how *that* must be clogging up his sieves.

"One thing I am glad about, though," Marie said after a pause, "is that since my return from Europe I have not yet come across a Marico girl who wears a selon's rose in her hair to make herself look more attractive to a young man – as happens time after time in Oom Schalk's stories."

This remark of Marie's gave a new turn to the conversation, and I felt relieved. For a moment I had feared that Marie Dupreez was also becoming addicted to the kind of Bushveld conversation that she complained about, and that she, too, was beginning to say the same thing over and over again.

Several women started talking, after that, about how hard it was to get flowers to grow in the Marico, on account of the prolonged droughts. The most they could hope for was to keep a bush of selon's roses alive near the kitchen door. It was a flower that seemed, if anything, to thrive on harsh sunlight and soapy dishwater and Marico earth, the women said.

Some time later we learnt that Theunis Dupreez, Marie's father, was giving up active farming, because of his rheumatics. We said, of course, that we knew how he had got his rheumatics. Through having spent so much time in all kinds of weather, we said, walking about the vlei in search of a new kind of sticky soil to put through his sieves.

Consequently, Theunis Dupreez engaged a young fellow, Joachem Bonthuys, to come and work on his farm as a bywoner. Joachem was a nephew of Philippus Bonthuys, and I was at the post office when he arrived at Drogedal, on the lorry from Zeerust, with Theunis Dupreez and his daughter, Marie, there to meet him.

Joachem Bonthuys's appearance was not very prepossessing, I thought. He shook hands somewhat awkwardly with the farmers who had come to meet the lorry to collect their milk-cans. Joachem did not seem to have much to say for himself, either, until Theunis Dupreez, his new employer, asked him what his journey up from Zeerust had been like.

"The veld is dry all the way," he replied. "And I've never seen so much heart-water in Afrikaner herds. They should dip their cattle every seven days."

Joachem Bonthuys spoke at great length, then, and I could not help smiling to myself when I saw Marie Dupreez turn away. In that moment my feelings also grew warmer towards Joachem. I felt that, at all events, he was not the kind of young man who would go and sing foreign songs under a respectable Boer girl's window.

All this brings me back to what I was saying about an old song and an old story. For it was quite a while before I again had occasion to visit the Dupreez farm. And when I sat smoking on the stoep with Theunis Dupreez it was just like an old story to hear him talk about his rheumatics.

Marie came out on to the stoep with a tray to bring us our coffee. – Yes, you've heard all that before, the same sort of thing. The same stoep. The same tray. – And for that reason, when she held the glass bowl out towards me, Marie Dupreez apologised for the yellow sugar.

"It's full of Kalahari sand, Oom Schalk," she said. "It's that Indian at Ramoutsa."

And when she turned to go back into the kitchen, leaving the two old men to their stories, it was not difficult for me to guess who the young man was for whom she was wearing a selon's rose pinned in her dark hair.

When the Heart is Eager

It was a visit that I remembered for the rest of my life (Oom Schalk Lourens said).

I was a small child, then. My father and his brother took me along in the back seat of the Cape-cart when they went to see an old man with a white beard. And when this old man stooped down to shake hands with me they told me to say, "Goeie dag, Oom Gysbert." I thought Oom Gysbert had something to do with God. I thought so from his voice and from Bible pictures I had seen of holy men, like prophets, who wore the same kind of beards.

My father and uncle went to see Oom Gysbert about pigs, which it seemed that he bred. And afterwards, when we drove home again, and my father and uncle spoke of Oom Gysbert, they both said he was a real old Pharisee. From that I was satisfied that I had been right in thinking of Oom Gysbert as a Bible person.

"Saying that those measled animals he sent us were the same prize pigs we had bought and paid for," my uncle went on, while we were riding back in the Cape-cart. "Does he not know how Ananias was smitten by the Lord?"

But that was not the reason why I remembered our visit to Oom Gysbert. For while I was on his farm I saw no pigs, measled or otherwise. And later in life I was to come across many more people that I have heard compared to Bible characters. To Judas, for instance.

After I had shaken hands with Oom Gysbert, the three men walked off together in the direction of the pigsties. I was left alone there, at the side of the house, where there was a stream of brown water flowing over rounded stones. This in itself was a sufficiently strange circumstance. You know how dry it is in these parts. I had until then seen water only in a dam or being pumped out of a borehole into a cattle-trough. I had never before in my life seen a stream of water flowing away over stones.

I learnt afterwards that Oom Gysbert's farm was near the Molopo, and that he was thus enabled to lead off furrows of water, except in the times of most severe drought, to irrigate his tilled lands. My father and uncle had left me by one of those water-furrows.

That was something I did not know then, of course.

I walked for some little distance downstream, paddling in the water, since I was bare-footed. Then it was that I came across a sight that I have never since forgotten. I had, of course, before then seen flowers. Veld flowers. And the moepel and the maroela in bloom. But that was the first time in my life that I had seen such pink and white flowers, growing in such amazing profusion, climbing over and covering a fence of wire-netting that seemed very high and that stretched away as far as I could see.

I could not explain then, any more than I can now, the feelings of joy that came to me when I stood by that fence where rambling roses clustered.

At intervals, from the direction of the pigsties, came the voices of my father and my uncle and Oom Gysbert, who were conversing. They were quite far away, for I could not see them. But they were conversing to each other very clearly, as though each thought that the other could perhaps not hear very well. Oom Gysbert was saying mostly, "Prize Large Whites," and my father and uncle were saying mostly, "Measled walking rubbish."

Afterwards it seemed that Oom Gysbert's wife had gone across to the pigsties, too. For I could hear a woman's voice starting to converse as well. She conversed even more distinctly than the men. So much so, that when a native passed where I was standing by the roses, he shook his head at me. For Oom Gysbert's wife had likewise begun by saying mostly, "Prize Large Whites." But she also ended up by saying, "Measled walking rubbish." And from the way the native shook his head it appeared that she wasn't talking about the pigs that Oom Gysbert had sold to my father and my uncle.

Meanwhile, I stood there by the fence, in childhood wonderment at all that loveliness. It was getting on towards evening. And all the air was filled with the fragrance of the roses. And there was the feeling that goes with wet earth. And a few pink and white petals floated in the brown water that rippled about my feet.

I was thrilled at this new strangeness and freshness of the world. And I thought that I would often again know the same kind of thrill.

But I never did.

Perhaps it is that as we grow older our senses do not get swayed by the perfume of flowers as much as they did when we were young. Or maybe it is that flowers just haven't got the same perfume anymore.

I realised that when I met Magda Burgers.

I should explain that my father gave up farming in that part of the

Marico a few years after his conversation with Oom Gysbert. My father said that the Bushveld was suited only for pigs. Hypocritical pigs with long white beards, my father took pains to make clear. So we went to the Highveld. Afterwards we trekked back to the Marico.

For in the meantime my father had found that the Highveld was good only for snakes. Snakes in the grass, who said one thing to you when they meant another, my father pointed out.

And years later I went to settle north of the Dwarsberge. Everything had changed a great deal, however, from when I had lived there as a child. People had died or trekked away. Strangers had come in and taken their places. Landmarks had grown unrecognisable.

Then, one day, I met Magda Burgers. I had gone over to Willem Burgers's farm with the intention of staying only long enough to borrow some mealie sacks. When I saw his daughter, Magda, I forgot what I had come about. This was all the more remarkable since the colour of Magda's hair kept on reminding me over and over again of ripe mealies. I stayed until quite late, and before leaving I had promised Willem Burgers that I would vote for him at the next Dwarsberg school committee elections.

I went to call on Willem Burgers often after that. My pretext was that I wanted to know still better why I should not vote for the other school committee candidates.

He told me. And I thought it was a pity that my father was not still alive to hear Willem Burgers talk. It would have done my father's heart good for him to know that he had been quite right when he said of the bush country that it was fit only for pigs with white beards. Willem Burgers also brought in pigs with brown beards and black beards, as well as a sprinkling of pigs that were clean-shaven. Willem Burgers also compared several of his rival candidates with persons in the Bible. I felt glad, then, that I had not also allowed my name to go forward the time they were taking nominations for the school committee.

Magda Burgers was in her early twenties. She was gay. There was something in her prettiness that in a strange way eluded me, also. And for this reason, I suppose, I was attracted to her more than ever.

But my real trouble was that I had little opportunity of talking to Magda alone.

I felt that she was not completely indifferent to me. I could tell that in a number of ways. There was, for instance, the afternoon when she allowed me to turn the handle of the cream separator for her in the milk-shed. That was very pleasant. The only difficulty was that I had to stand sideways. For it was a small shed. And Willem Burgers took up most of the room, sitting on an upturned bucket. He was busy telling me that Gerhardus Oosthuizen was like a hyena.

Another time, Magda allowed me to dry the cups for her in the kitchen when she washed up after we had had coffee. But the kitchen was also small, and her father took up a lot of space, sitting on an upturned paraffin box. He was then engaged in explaining to me that Flip Welman was like a green tree-snake with black spots on his behind. Nevertheless, each time Magda Burgers passed me a spoon to dry, I was able to hold her hand for a few moments. Once she was so absent-minded as to pass me her hand even when there wasn't a spoon in it.

But during all these weeks I was never able to speak to Magda Burgers on her own. And always there was something in her prettiness that eluded me.

Then, one afternoon, when Magda's father was telling me that 'Rooi' François Hanekom was like a crocodile with laced-up top-boots and a gold chain on his belly, two men came to the door. They were strangers to me. I could not remember Willem Burgers having mentioned them to me, either, as resembling some of the more unsatisfactory sort of Bushveld animal. From this I concluded that they were not candidates for the school committee.

Magda told me that the visitors were the Van Breda brothers.

"The tall one with the cleft in his chin is Joost van Breda," she said.

Willem Burgers walked off with the two men along a footpath that led to the back of the house.

That was how, for the first time, I came to find myself alone with Magda. And because she looked so beautiful to me, then, with a light in her eyes that I thought not to have seen there before, I told her of my visit to a farm, long ago, in the company of my father and my uncle. I told her of how I stood by a fence covered in roses, where there was a stream of brown water. I spoke of the rose perfume that had enchanted me as a child, and that I had not known since. It seems queer to me, now, that I was able to say so much to her, all in a few minutes.

I also said a few more words to her in a voice that I could not keep steady.

"Oom Gysbert?" Magda asked. "Why, it must be this same farm. Years ago this farm belonged to an old Gysbert Steenkamp. Come, I will show you."

Magda led me out of the house along a path which was different from the footpath her father and the Van Breda brothers had taken, and which was not the way, either, to the milk-shed.

It was getting on towards sunset. In the west the sky was gaudy with stripes like a native blanket. In the distance we could hear the voices of Magda's father and the Van Breda brothers raised in conversation. It was all just like long ago. Before I realised it I found I had taken Magda's hand.

"I suppose they are talking about pigs," I said to Magda. And I laughed, remembering that other day, which did not seem so far off, then, when I was a child.

"Yes," Magda answered. "Joost van Breda – the one with the cleft in his chin – bought some pigs from my father last month."

Even before we got there, I knew it was the same place. I could sense it all in a single moment, and without knowing how.

A few yards further on I came across that fence. It did not look at all high, anymore. But it was clustered about with pink and white roses that grew in great profusion, climbing over and covering the netting for almost as far as I could see.

Before I reached the fence, however, Magda Burgers had left me. She had slipped her small white hand out of mine and had sped off through the trees into the gathering dusk – and in the direction from which came the voices of her father and the two Van Breda brothers. The three men were conversing very clearly, by then, as though each thought the other was deaf. The Van Breda brothers were also laughing very distinctly. They laughed every time Magda's father said, "Prize Large Whites." And after they laughed they used rough language.

A little later a girl's voice started joining in the conversation. And I did not need a native to come by and shake his head at me. It was a sad enough thing for me, in any case, to have to listen to a young girl taking the part of two strangers against her father. She sided particularly with one of the two strangers. I knew, without having to be told, that the stranger was tall and had a cleft in his chin.

I stood for a long time watching the brown water flowing along the furrow. And I thought of how much water had flowed down all the rivers and under all the bridges of the world since I had last stood on that spot, as a child.

The roses clambering over the wire-netting shed no heady perfumes.

The Brothers

It is true saying that man may scheme, but that God has the last word (Oom Schalk Lourens said).

And it was no different with Krisjan Lategan. He had one aim, and that was to make sure that his farm should remain the home of the Lategans from one generation to the next until the end of the world. This would be in about two hundred years, according to the way in which a church elder, who was skilled in Biblical prophecy, had worked it out. It would be on a Sunday morning.

Krisjan Lategan wanted his whole family around him, so that they could all stand up together on the Last Day. There was to be none of that rushing around to look for Lategans who had wandered off into distant parts. Especially with the Last Day being a Sunday and all. Krisjan Lategan was particular that a solemn occasion should not be spoilt by the bad language that always went with searching for stray cattle on a morning when you had to trek.

Afterwards, when they brought the telegraph up as far as Nietverdiend, and they showed the church elder how it worked, the elder said that he did not give the world a full two hundred years anymore. And when in Zeerust he heard a talking machine that could sing songs and speak words just through your turning a handle, the elder said that the end of the world was now quite near.

And he said it almost as though he was glad.

It was then that old Krisjan Lategan set about the construction of the family vault at the end of his farm. It was the kind of vault that you see on some farms in the Cape. There was a low wall round it, like for a sheep fold, and the vault was only a few feet below the level of the ground, and you walked down steps to a wooden door fastened with a chain. Inside were tamboetie-wood trestles for the coffins to go on. The trestles were painted with tar, to keep away the white ants.

It was a fine vault. Farmers came from many miles away to admire it. And, as always happens in such cases, after their first feelings of awe had worn off, the visitors would make remarks which, in the parts of the Marico near the Bechuanaland border, regularly aroused guffaws.

They said, yes, it was quite a nice house, but where was the chimney? They also said that if you got up in the middle of the night and reached your hand under the bed – well, the vault wasn't a properly fixed-up kind of vault at all.

The remark Hans van Tonder made was also regarded as having a lot of class to it. Referring to the tar on the trestles, he said he couldn't understand why old Krisjan Lategan should be so fussy about keeping the white ants out. "When you lie in your coffin, it's not by *ants* that you get eaten up," Hans van Tonder said.

Krisjan Lategan's neighbours had a lot of things of this nature to say about his vault when it was newly constructed. All the same, not one of them would have been anxious to go to the vault alone at night after Krisjan Lategan had been laid to rest in it.

And yet all Krisjan Lategan's plans came to nothing. Shortly after his death certain unusual events occurred on his farm, as a result of which one of his two sons came to an untimely end, and his corpse was placed in the vault in a coffin that was much too long. And the other son fled so far out of the Marico that it would certainly not be possible to find him again before the Last Day. And even then, on the Day of Judgement, he would not be likely to push himself to the front to any extent.

Everybody in the Bushveld knew of the bitterness that there was between old Krisjan Lategan's two sons, Doors and Lodewyk, who were in all things so unlike each other. At their father's death the two brothers were in their twenties. Neither was married. Doors was a few years older than Lodewyk. For a long time the only bond between them seemed to have been their mutual enmity.

Lodewyk, the younger one, was tall and good-looking, and his nature was adventurous. The elder brother, Doors, was a hunchback. He had short legs and unnaturally broad shoulders. He was credited with great strength. Because of his grotesque shape, the natives told stories about him that had to do with witchcraft, and that could not be true.

At his father's funeral Doors, with his short stature and the shapeless hump on his back, looked particularly ungainly among the other pall-bearers, all straight and upstanding men. During the simple service before the open doors of the vault a child burst out crying. It was something of a scandal that the child wept out of terror of Doors Lategan's hunched figure, and not out of sorrow for the departed.

Soon afterwards Lodewyk Lategan left the farm for the diamond diggings at Doornpan. Before that the brothers had quarrelled violently in the mealie-lands. The natives said that the quarrel had been about what cattle Lodewyk could take with him to the diggings. When Lodewyk went it was with the new wagon and the best span of oxen. And Doors said that if he ever returned to the farm he would kill him.

"I will yet make you remember those words," Lodewyk answered.

In this spirit Doors and Lodewyk parted. Tant Alie, old Krisjan Lategan's widow, remained on at the farm with her elder son, Doors. She was an ageing woman with no force of character. Tant Alie had always been considered a bit soft in the head. She came of a Cape family of which quite a few members were known to be 'simpel', although nobody, of course, thought any the less of them on that account. They belonged to a sheep district, Tant Alie's family, and we of the Marico, who were cattle farmers, said that for a sheep farmer it was even a help if his brain was not too sound.

But whatever Tant Alie might have thought and felt about the estrangement that was between her sons, she did not ever discuss the matter. Moreover it is certain that they would have taken no notice of any efforts on her part at reconciling them.

Lodewyk left for the diamond fields in the company of Flippie Geel, who had a piece of Government land at Koedoesrand that he was supposed to improve. Flippie Geel was a good deal older than Lodewyk Lategan. For that reason it seems all the more surprising that he should have helped Lodewyk in his subsequent foolish actions. Perhaps it was because Flippie Geel found that easier than work.

From what came out afterwards, it would appear that Lodewyk Lategan and Flippie Geel did not dig much on their claim. But they put in a lot of time drinking brandy, which they bought with the money Lodewyk got from selling his trek-oxen, a pair at a time.

And when he was in his cups, Lodewyk would devise elaborate schemes, each more absurd than the last, for getting even with his brother Doors, who, he said, had defrauded him of his share of the inheritance.

After he had rejected a number of ideas, one after the other, as impracticable, Lodewyk got hold of a plan that he decided to carry out. From this you can get some sort of conception as to how crackbrained those plans must have been that he didn't act on. Anyway, he got Flippie Geel to write to Doors to tell him that his brother Lodewyk had been killed in an accident on the diggings, and that his body was being sent home in a coffin by transport wagon. And a few days later a coffin, which Lodewyk had had made to his size, was on its way to the Lategan farm. Inside the coffin, instead of a corpse, was a mealie-sack that Lodewyk and Flippie Geel had filled with gravel. I suppose that was the only time, too, that they had a spade in their hands during their stay on the diggings.

Now, I have often tried to puzzle out – and so have many other people: for although it all happened long ago this story is still well known hereabouts – what idea Lodewyk Lategan had with that coffin. For one thing, he was drunk very often during that period. And he no doubt also inherited a good deal of his mother's weakness of mind. But he must surely have expected Doors to unscrew the lid of the coffin, if for no other reason than just to make certain that Lodewyk really was dead.

He could surely not have foreseen Doors acting the way he did when the coffin was delivered on the front stoep of the Lategan homestead. Without getting up from the riempies chair on which he was sitting – well forward because of his hump – Doors shouted for the farm natives to come and fetch away the coffin.

"The key of the vault is hanging on the wall of the voorkamer," Doors said. "Unlock the vault and put this box on one of the trestles. Close the doors but don't put the lock on the chain again."

Doors silenced his mother roughly when she tried to speak. Tant Alie had wanted to be allowed to gaze for the last time on the face of her dead son.

The transport driver, who had helped to carry the coffin on to the stoep and had stood bare-headed beside it in reverence for the dead, walked back to his team a very amazed man.

There were some, however, who say that Doors Lategan had second sight. Or if it wasn't second sight it was a depth of cunning that was even better than second sight. And that he had guessed that his brother Lodewyk's body was not in the coffin.

The farmers of the neighbourhood had naturally no suspicions of this nature, however. Many of them sent wreaths.

A few weeks later it was known that Lodewyk's ghost was haunting the Lategan farm. Several natives testified to having seen the ghost of Baas Lodewyk on a couple of moonlight nights. They had seen Baas Lodewyk's ghost by the vault, they said. Baas Lodewyk's ghost was sitting on the low wall and there was what looked like a black bottle in his hand. One man also said that he thought Baas Lodewyk's ghost was singing. But he couldn't be certain on that point. He didn't want to make sure, the native said.

But what were even better authenticated were the times when Lodewyk's ghost was seen driving along the high road in the back of Flippie Geel's mule-cart that had a half-hood over the back seat. Even white people had seen Lodewyk's ghost riding in the back seat of Flippie Geel's mule-cart. It was known that Flippie Geel had recently returned to the Marico to improve his Government land some more. He had already sold the mealie-planter that he had got on loan from the Government. He was now trying to sell the disc-plough with green handles.

Because in life Lodewyk Lategan had been Flippie Geel's bosom friend, it was not surprising, people said, that Lodewyk's ghost should have been seen in the back of Flippie Geel's mule-cart. But they were glad for Flippie's sake that Flippie hadn't turned round. Lodewyk's ghost looked too awful, the people said who saw it. It was almost as though it was trying to hide itself away against the half-hood of the cart.

It was when an inquisitive farmer crept up on the window of Flippie Geel's rondavel, one evening, and saw Lodewyk's ghost sitting with its feet on the table, eating biltong, that the truth came out. Next day everybody in the Marico knew that Lodewyk Lategan was not dead.

Shortly afterwards came the night when Doors's natives reported to him that they had seen Baas Lodewyk climbing through the barbed wire with a gun in his hands. Doors took down his Mauser from the wall and strode out into the veld.

Except for the few shots during the night, everything on the farm next day seemed as it had been before. The only difference was that in the Lategan family vault a sack of gravel in a coffin had been replaced by a body, and the lid of the coffin had been screwed on again. During the night one brother had been murdered. And the other had fled. He was never caught.

Several days passed before the veldkornet came to the Lategan farm. And then Tant Alie would not give him permission to open the coffin.

"One of my sons is in the vault and the other is a fugitive over the face of the earth," Tant Alie said. "I don't want to know which is which."

Nevertheless, the veldkornet had his way. He came back with an official paper and unscrewed the lid. In the coffin that was much too long for him – although it was cramped for breadth – lay Doors, the hunchback brother, with a bullet in his heart.

But even before the veldkornet opened the coffin it was known in the Marico that it was Doors that had been murdered. For when Lodewyk Lategan fled from the Marico he drove off in Flippie Geel's mule-cart. Several people had seen Lodewyk driving along the highway in the night. And those people said that for Lodewyk's own sake they were glad that Lodewyk did not look round.

It was as well for Lodewyk Lategan, they said, that he should drive off and not know that there was a passenger in the back seat. The passenger had broad shoulders and the starlight shone through his ungainly hump.

Oom Piet's Party

All the young people of the Dwarsberge were at Piet van Zyl's party, that night. Also some people that weren't perhaps so very young. And they had come, some of them, from even further than the Dwarsberge. They explained, a couple of what you can call the more elderly guests, that it was not the thought of Piet van Zyl's moepel brandy that had brought them all that way. For that matter, as Willem Pretorius said, he for his part had not been invited, even. And then Bart Lemmer said that for his part, he had not been invited either, but he had come along there, to Piet van Zyl's farmhouse, in the evening, because Piet van Zyl's farmhouse stood so high up, against Tsalala's Kop, and it would be good for his asthma, to be so high up, for a change. Then Willem Pretorius said that it was something in some part of his spine that was being done good. But he didn't say what with.

Piet van Zyl had taken a lot of trouble over that party. He had cleared all the furniture out of the voorhuis except two chairs for the Bester brothers to sit on with their concertina and guitar, and a tall tamboetie kist that a guest who wasn't dancing could stand and rest his elbows on. In the kitchen there were bottles and jars on a long table.

Wynand Smit was explaining what the exact kind of illness was that had brought him along to the dance, when Willem Pretorius interrupted him.

"Look, kêrels," Willem Pretorius said. "This is, after all, a dance. Let us not be so unsociable as to remain standing here talking on the stoep on our own about our sicknesses."

Bart Lemmer and Wynand Smit agreed with him. He had also been thinking of going into the kitchen, Bart Lemmer said.

On the way to the kitchen they had to pass through the voorkamer where there were young men in shirt-sleeves and young girls in pretty coloured dresses dancing in lively fashion.

"I think I will come back a little later here, and dance," Willem Pretorius said, on the way to the kitchen.

Bart Lemmer said he thought he would, too, when it was a bit cooler, and he didn't need to take his jacket off. It would appear that he had dressed somewhat hurriedly for the dance and had neglected to change the shirt in which he had climbed through a barbed-wire fence a week before, a few yards ahead of a bull.

These smart young men of today, with their striped shirts and their ties with big yellow flowers on, were much too fussy, Wynand Smit acknowledged.

They reached the kitchen just at the moment when the outside door was being opened and Lettie van Zyl, the wife of the host, came in, followed by two Mtosas, who carried between them a dish that was almost the size of a small bath. From the remarks the one Mtosa was making about the way the other Mtosa was not looking where he was going, one gathered that the dish was hot.

"I always say that's the best way to cook, Nig Lettie," Willem Pretorius said to Piet van Zyl's wife in a friendly fashion. "You can't beat the old bakoond of sun-dried brick. That's what I say. And I can see, from what's inside the dish, that you have still got ribbokke under those rante."

By that time both Mtosas were making remarks. They wanted to get the dish on to the kitchen table, and Bart Lemmer was standing in the way. Wynand Smit saw what the difficulty was and stepped forward to help the Mtosas. The dish nearly fell on the floor, then, from the sudden way Wynand Smit jumped when he let go.

"If I had known it was so hot I would have got a rag," he said in sombre tones, looking at his hands.

"All the same, I am surprised," Lettie van Zyl said to Willem Pretorius.

"Ag, think nothing of it, Niggie," Willem Pretorius replied. "We are all Bushveld farmers. And for some special time, like this dance, ah, well, even if ribbok *is* royal game, nobody will think anything – "

"That wasn't what I was talking about," Lettie said quickly, coming to the point. "I am surprised to see you here at the dance. Not that you aren't very welcome, of course, Neef Willem. Don't think that. You and Neef Bart and Neef Wynand – Piet and I are naturally glad to have you. But I mean, after what happened last time – "

"Oh, that?" Willem Pretorius asked, affecting surprise. "But how was I to know that that man with the black beard was an ouderling? He wasn't wearing a manel. All I saw was a man wearing a black beard. And even if he wore a manel, I don't think it was the right sort of a place for an ouderling to be. With dancing – and – and singing – and – and *drinking* – "

"But the ouderling did not dance," Lettie van Zyl replied. "And all he drank was coffee."

Willem Pretorius looked sceptical.

"Well, all I can say," he said, "is that if he wasn't drunk, how did he come to fall into the dam?"

Lettie van Zyl started going out of the kitchen to find out whether her guests would like to eat now or a little later. When she got to the door she turned round and faced Willem Pretorius with a look conveying a sort of finality.

"It wasn't the ouderling that fell into the dam, Neef Willem," she said. "It was you that fell in."

Willem Pretorius kept on insisting, but not very loudly, that a Bushveld party was *still* no place for an ouderling to come dancing and singing and – and *swearing* in.

"Royal game," Piet van Zyl, the host, said. Piet van Zyl was leaning against the tall tamboetie kist in the corner, talking to a small group standing around him with plates. "Royal game is about all we got left to shoot for the bakoond, these days. That's all since the time the game got protected by law. I am not allowed to shoot a ribbok here on my own farm, anymore, because of the law. So that's about all we've got to eat here, today, in the way of wildevleis. And not too much of that, either. And yet I can remember the time when game swarmed around Tsalala's Kop almost like in the Kruger Park. That was before a lot of Volksraad members who just sit and talk and call each other names got hold of the idea that they had to protect the game in the Bushveld by law. Protect them against what? That's what I want to know."

Several members of the little group said he was quite right. Yes, they said, also against what?

"And what's the result today?" Piet van Zyl demanded. "Why, today, about all the game that's left are a few ribbokke in the rante. And all that's just *since* these game laws. They say they've got the game laws for protecting the animals in the Kruger Park, also. Well, if that's so, I won't give much for the chances of the Kruger Park, that's all."

Piet van Zyl's logic made a strong appeal to most of the members of his small audience. Young Dawie Gouws started telling a story that his grandfather told him out of his own mouth about the time Dawie Gouws's grandfather shot a whole herd of elephants that had got knee-deep into the swampy ground by the Molopo.

"And where are those herds of elephants today?" Dawie Gouws asked. "It's all these politicians with their game laws. Why, there is hardly a single elephant left by the Molopo, today."

Piet van Zyl said that, everything considered, it wasn't surprising.

"I got this ribbok at about four hundred yards," Piet van Zyl went on, "just as he was disappearing into a clump of kameeldorings. About a mile from there, on my way home, when I put the ribbok down to rest again, I got an aardvark just as he was disappearing into his hole. I got him at about two hundred yards."

Meneer Strydom, the new schoolmaster, asked Piet van Zyl what he wanted to do that sort of thing for. We called him Meneer Strydom because he called everyone else Meneer, instead of Neef or Oom or Swaer. The schoolmaster was from the city.

"I have read all about the aardvark in a book on natural history," Meneer Strydom went on. "Did you know that the aardvark is the friend of man? I can't understand this senseless lust for destruction – just so that you can say afterwards that you got an animal at so many hundred yards. I mean, nobody has got a greater admiration for a big game hunter than I have – at a suitable distance, and with the wind blowing in the wrong direction, so that he can't smell me. And I would like to be among trees, the trunks of which at a distance you would confuse my flannel trousers with."

Piet van Zyl said he had thought of that before today. The schoolmaster must not think he had not thought of that before today. But if it was an early winter morning and there was a slight breeze blowing, and there was mist on the rante, then he wouldn't mind if he shot a rhinoceros, on such a morning. And if he couldn't get a rhinoceros, then a baboon would do, perhaps. He didn't say that he would feel like that later in the day, now. He had hardly ever gone out hunting later in the day – just mornings and evenings. It wasn't as though he hadn't thought of such things, but that was how it was. It must be some sort of instinct.

"Well, I am glad I haven't got that sort of instinct," Meneer Strydom said. And when Lettie van Zyl came to offer him another thick slice of roast ribbok he declined quite pointedly. He might have a little afterwards, though, he said, with bread and butter.

It was queer how, for a spell, Piet van Zyl's talk of hunting got everybody interested in the subject to the exclusion of the dancing and even of the mampoer. A young man would forget the girl dancing in his arms to the vastrap tune of "Die Wilde Weduwee van Windhoek" and would start demonstrating to another young man how he shot that tree-full of sleeping tarentale.

At one stage the elder Bester brother put down his concertina and started kneeling on the floor, bending forward. It looked as though a piece of his concertina had got lost and he was looking for it on the floor.

But it was only when the younger Bester brother also stopped playing for a bit, and the elder Bester took up the guitar that his younger brother had put down and, still kneeling, pointed with it, that you knew what he was saying.

You didn't have to hear the words.

Meneer Strydom slipped through into the kitchen. In the kitchen Willem Pretorius was kneeling half under the table. Having already heard the elder Bester brother, Meneer Strydom knew what was coming.

"And there was the lion crouching," Willem Pretorius was saying, "ready to – "

While helping himself to a drink, Meneer Strydom took the opportunity of explaining to Bart Lemmer that the despised earthworm was in reality the friend of man. Because Meneer Strydom was a schoolteacher, Bart Lemmer took it in good part.

"What I say," Bart Lemmer said to Wynand Smit, however, after Meneer Strydom had gone back into the voorkamer, "is that that schoolmaster must have pretty queer friends. Next thing he'll be saying that the boomslang and the Klipkop Mshangaan are also the friend of man."

"On with the dance," the younger Bester brother called out, taking his guitar away from his elder brother, who was getting ready to reload, to the impairment of the G-string. Soon afterwards the interlude of the huntsman was forgotten. Dust from the swift feet of the dancers rose up once more to the ceiling. Outside there shone the moon that in the past had seen great herds making their way to the water. Old vanished herds.

There was a shot. The music and the dancing ceased. Two more shots in quick succession.

"Poachers from the city," Piet van Zyl declared, his face pale with fury in the candlelight. "Coming here with motor cars. And we can't do anything about it. By the time we get there they will be gone. Bloodthirsty savages from the city coming here to exterminate our wildlife."

We agreed with Piet van Zyl that it was no good going after those poachers. They were sure to be gone. There was also the possibility – although we did not say that to each other openly – that those savages with their senseless bloodlust, and so quick on the trigger in the dark, and all, just might not *be* gone.

Only Willem Pretorius went out to see. Bart Lemmer and Wynand Smit followed him, staggering slightly. A little later we heard evil sounds. But it was not an encounter with poachers. When Bart and Wynand came back they said it was enough they had done in pulling Willem Pretorius out. His hat they would go and look for in the dam in the morning.

The Missionary

That kaffir carving on the wall of my voorkamer (Oom Schalk Lourens said), it's been there for many years. It was found in the loft of the pastorie at Ramoutsa after the death of the Dutch Reformed missionary there, Reverend Keet.

To look at, it's just one of those figures that a kaffir wood-carver cuts out of soft wood, like mdubu or mesetla. But because I knew him quite well, I can still see a rough sort of resemblance to Reverend Keet in that carving, even though it is now discoloured with age and the white ants have eaten away parts of it. I first saw this figure in the study of the pastorie at Ramoutsa when I went to call on Reverend Keet. And when, after his death, the carving was found in the loft of the pastorie, I brought it here. I kept it in memory of a man who had strange ideas about what he was pleased to call Darkest Africa.

Reverend Keet had not been at Ramoutsa very long. Before that he had worked at a mission station in the Cape. But, as he told us, ever since he had paid a visit to the Marico District, some years before, he had wanted to come to the Western Transvaal. He said he had obtained, in the Bushveld along the Molopo River, a feeling that here was the real Africa. He said there was a spirit of evil in these parts that he believed it was his mission to overcome.

We who had lived in the Marico for the greater part of our lives wondered what we had done to him.

On his previous visit here Reverend Keet had stayed long enough to meet Elsiba Grobler, the daughter of Thys Grobler of Drogedal. Afterwards he had sent for Elsiba to come down to the Cape to be his bride.

And so we thought that the missionary had remembered with affection the scenes that were the setting for his courtship. And that was why he came back here. So you can imagine how disappointed we were in learning the truth.

Nevertheless, I found it interesting to listen to him, just because he had such outlandish views. And so I called on him quite regularly when I passed the mission station on my way back from the Indian store at Ramoutsa.

Reverend Keet and I used to sit in his study, where the curtains were half drawn, as they were in the whole pastorie. I supposed it was to keep out the bright sunshine that Darkest Africa is so full of.

"Only yesterday a kaffir child hurt his leg falling out of a withaak tree," Reverend Keet said to me on one occasion. "And the parents didn't bring the child here so that Elsiba or I could bandage him up. Instead, they said there was a devil in the withaak. And so they got the witch-doctor to fasten a piece of crocodile skin to the child's leg, to drive away the devil."

So I said that that just showed you how ignorant a kaffir was. They should have fastened the crocodile skin to the withaak, instead, like the old people used to do. That would drive the devil away quick enough, I said.

Reverend Keet did not answer. He just shook his head and looked at me in a pitying sort of way, so that I felt sorry I had spoken.

To change the subject I pointed to a kaffir wood-carving standing on a table in the corner of the study. That same wood-carving you see today hanging on the wall of my voorkamer.

"Here's now something that we want to encourage," Reverend Keet said in answer to my question. "Through art we can perhaps bring enlightenment to these parts. The kaffirs here seem to have a natural talent for wood-carving. I have asked Willem Terreblanche to write to the Education Department for a text-book on the subject. It will be another craft that we can teach to the children at the school."

Willem Terreblanche was the assistant teacher at the mission station.

"Anyway, it will be more useful than that last text-book we got on how to make paper serviettes with tassels," Reverend Keet went on, half to himself. Then it was as though an idea struck him. "Oh, by the way," he asked, "would you perhaps like, say, a few dozen paper serviettes with tassels to take home with you?"

I declined his offer in some haste.

Reverend Keet started talking about that carving again.

"You wouldn't think it was meant for me, now, would you?" he asked.

And because I am always polite, that way, I said no, certainly not.

"I mean, just look at the top of the body," he said. "It's like a sack of potatoes. Does the top part of my body look like a sack of potatoes?"

And once again I said no, oh no.

Reverend Keet laughed, then – rather loudly I thought – at the idea of the wood-carver's ignorance. I laughed quite loudly, also, to make it clear that I, too, thought that the kaffir wood-carver was very ignorant.

"All the same, for a raw kaffir who has had no training," the missionary continued, "it's not bad. But take that self-satisfied sort of smile, now, that he put on my face. It only came out that way because the kaffir who made the carving lacks the skill to carve my features as they really are. He hasn't got technique."

I thought, well, maybe that ignorant Bechuana didn't know any more what technique was than I did. But I did think he had a pretty shrewd idea how to carve a wooden figure of Reverend Keet.

"If a kaffir had the impudence to make a likeness like that of me, with such big ears and all," I said to Reverend Keet, "I would kick him in the ribs. I would kick him for being so ignorant, I mean."

It was then that Elsiba brought us in our coffee. Although she was now the missionary's wife, I still thought of her as Elsiba, a Bushveld girl whom I had seen grow up.

"You've still got that thing there," Elsiba said to her husband, after she had greeted me. "I won't have you making a fool of yourself. Every visitor to the pastorie who sees this carving goes away laughing at you."

"They laugh at the kaffir who made it, Elsiba, because of his poor technique," Reverend Keet said, drawing himself up in his chair.

"Anyway, I'm taking it out of here," Elsiba answered.

I have since then often thought of that scene. Of the way Elsiba Keet walked from the room, with the carving standing upright on the tray that she had carried the coffee-cups on. Because of its big feet that wooden figure did not fall over when Elsiba flounced out with the tray. And in its stiff, wooden bearing the figure seemed to be expressing the same disdain of the kaffir wood-carver's technique as what Reverend Keet had.

I remained in the study a long time. And all the while the missionary talked of the spirit of evil that hung over the Marico like a heavy blanket. It was something brooding and oppressive, he said, and it did something to the souls of men. He asked me whether I hadn't noticed it myself.

So I told him that I had. I said that he had taken the very words out of my mouth. And I proceeded to tell him about the time Jurie Bekker had impounded some of my cattle that he claimed had strayed into his mealie-lands.

"You should have seen Jurie Bekker the morning that he drove off my cattle along the Government Road," I said. "An evil blanket hung over him, all right. You could almost see it. A striped kaffir blanket."

I also told the missionary about the sinful way in which Niklaas Prinsloo had filled in those compensation forms for losses which he had never suffered, even. And about the time Gert Haasbroek sold me what he said was a pedigree Afrikaner bull, and that was just an animal he had smuggled through from the Protectorate one night, with a whole herd of other beasts, and that died afterwards of grass-belly.

I said that the whole of the Marico District was just bristling with evil, and I could give him many more examples, if he would care to listen.

But Reverend Keet said that was not what he meant. He said he was talking of the unnatural influences that hovered over this part of the country. He had felt those things particularly at the swamps by the Molopo, he said, with the green bubbles coming up out of the mud and with those trees that were like shapes oppressing your mind when it is fevered. But it was like that everywhere in the Bushveld, he said. With the sun pouring down at midday, for instance, and the whole veld very still, it was yet as though there was a high black wind, somewhere, an old lost wind. And he felt a chill in all his bones, he said, and it was something unearthly.

It was interesting for me to hear the Reverend Keet talk like that. I had heard the same sort of thing before from strangers. I wondered what he could take for it.

"Even here in this study, where I am sitting talking to you," he added, "I can sense a baleful influence. It is some form of – of something skulking, somehow."

I knew, of course, that Reverend Keet was not making any underhanded allusion to my being there in his study. He was too religious to do a thing like that. Nevertheless, I felt uncomfortable. Shortly afterwards I left.

On my way back in the mule-cart I passed the mission school. And I thought then that it was funny that Elsiba was so concerned that a kaffir should not make a fool of her husband with a wood-carving of him. Because she did not seem to mind making a fool of him in another way. From the mule-cart I saw Elsiba and Willem Terreblanche in the doorway of the schoolroom. And from the way they were holding hands I could see that they were not discussing paper serviettes with tassels, or any similar school subjects.

Still, as it turned out, it never came to any scandal in the district. For Willem Terreblanche left some time later to take up a teaching post in the Free State. And after Reverend Keet's death Elsiba allowed a respectable interval to elapse before she went to the Free State to marry Willem Terreblanche.

Some distance beyond the mission school I came across the Ramoutsa witch-doctor that Reverend Keet had spoken about. The witch-doctor was busy digging up roots on the veld for medicine. I reined in the mules and the witch-doctor came up to me. He had on a pair of brown leggings and a woman's corset. And he carried an umbrella. Around his neck he wore a few feet of light-green tree-snake that didn't look as though it had been dead very long. I could see that the witch-doctor was particular about how he dressed when he went out.

I spoke to him in Sechuana about Reverend Keet. I told him that Reverend Keet said the Marico was a bad place. I also told him that the missionary did not believe in the cure of fastening a piece of crocodile skin to the leg of a child who had fallen out of a withaak tree. And I said that he did not seem to think, either, that if you fastened crocodile skin to the withaak it would drive the devil out of it.

The witch-doctor stood thinking for some while. And when he spoke again it seemed to me that in his answer there was a measure of wisdom.

"The best thing," he said, "would be to fasten a piece of crocodile skin on to the baas missionary."

It seemed quite possible that the devils were not all just in the Marico Bushveld. There might be one or two inside Reverend Keet himself, also.

Nevertheless, I have often since then thought of how almost inspired Reverend Keet was when he said that there was evil going on around him, right here in the Marico. In his very home – he could have said. With the curtains half drawn and all. Only, of course, he didn't mean it that way.

Yet I have also wondered if, in the way he did mean it – when he spoke of those darker things that he claimed were at work in Africa – I wonder if there, too, Reverend Keet was as wide of the mark as one might lightly suppose.

That thought first occurred to me after Reverend Keet's death and Elsiba's departure. In fact, it was when the new missionary took over the pastorie at Ramoutsa and this wood-carving was found in the loft.

But before I hung up the carving where you see it now, I first took the trouble to pluck off the lock of Reverend Keet's hair that had been glued to it. And I also plucked out the nails that had been driven – by Elsiba's hands, I could not but think – into the head and heart.

Funeral Earth

We had a difficult task, that time (Oom Schalk Lourens said), teaching Sijefu's tribe of Mtosas to become civilised. But they did not show any appreciation. Even after we had set fire to their huts in a long row round the slopes of Abjaterskop, so that you could see the smoke almost as far as Nietverdiend, the Mtosas remained just about as unenlightened as ever. They would retreat into the mountains, where it was almost impossible for our commando to follow them on horseback. They remained hidden in the thick bush.

"I can sense these kaffirs all around us," Veldkornet Andries Joubert said to our seksie of about a dozen burghers when we had come to a halt in a clearing amid the tall withaaks. "I have been in so many kaffir wars that I can almost *smell* when there are kaffirs lying in wait for us with assegais. And yet all day long you never see a single Mtosa that you can put a lead bullet through."

He also said that if this war went on much longer we would forget altogether how to handle a gun. And what would we do then, when we again had to fight England?

Young Fanie Louw, who liked saying funny things, threw back his head and pretended to be sniffing the air with discrimination. "I can smell a whole row of assegais with broad blades and short handles," Fanie Louw said. "The stabbing assegai has got more of a selon's rose sort of smell about it than a throwing spear. The selon's rose that you come across in graveyards."

The veldkornet did not think Fanie Louw's remark very funny, however. And he said we all knew that this was the first time Fanie Louw had ever been on commando. He also said that if a crowd of Mtosas were to leap out of the bush on to us suddenly, then you wouldn't be able to smell Fanie Louw for dust. The veldkornet also said another thing that was even better.

Our group of burghers laughed heartily. Maybe Veldkornet Joubert could not think out a lot of nonsense to say just on the spur of the moment, in the way that Fanie Louw could, but give our veldkornet a chance to reflect, first, and he would come out with the kind of remark that you just had to admire.

Indeed, from the very next thing Veldkornet Joubert said, you could see how deep was his insight. And he did not have to think much, either, then.

"Let us get out of here as quick as hell, men," he said, speaking very distinctly. "Perhaps the kaffirs are hiding out in the open turf-lands, where there are no trees. And none of this long tamboekie grass, either."

When we emerged from that stretch of bush we were glad to discover that our veldkornet had been right, like always.

For another group of Transvaal burghers had hit on the same strategy.

"We were in the middle of the bush," their leader, Combrinck, said to us, after we had exchanged greetings. "A very thick part of the bush, with withaaks standing up like skeletons. And we suddenly thought the Mtosas might have gone into hiding out here in the open."

You could see that Veldkornet Joubert was pleased to think that he had, on his own, worked out the same tactics as Combrinck, who was known as a skilful kaffir-fighter. All the same, it seemed as though this was going to be a long war.

It was then that, again speaking out of his turn, Fanie Louw said that all we needed now was for the kommandant himself to arrive there in the middle of the turf-lands with the main body of burghers. "Maybe we should even go back to Pretoria to see if the Mtosas aren't perhaps hiding in the Volksraad," he said. "Passing laws and things. You know how cheeky a Mtosa is."

"It can't be worse than some of the laws that the Volksraad is already passing now," Combrinck said, gruffly. From that we could see that why he had not himself been appointed kommandant was because he had voted against the President in the last elections.

By that time the sun was sitting not more than about two Cape feet above a tall koppie on the horizon. Accordingly, we started looking about for a place to camp. It was muddy in the turf-lands, and there was no firewood there, but we all said that we did not mind. We would not pamper ourselves by going to sleep in the thick bush, we told one another. It was war-time, and we were on commando, and the mud of the turf-lands was good enough for *us*, we said.

It was then that an unusual thing happened.

For we suddenly did see Mtosas. We saw them from a long way off. They came out of the bush and marched right out into the open. They made no attempt to hide. We saw in amazement that they were coming straight in our direction, advancing in single file. And we observed, even from that distance, that they were unarmed. Instead of assegais and shields they carried burdens on their heads. And almost in that same moment we realised, from the heavy look of those burdens, that the carriers must be women.

For that reason we took our guns in our hands and stood waiting. Since it was women, we were naturally prepared for the lowest form of treachery.

As the column drew nearer we saw that at the head of it was Ndambe, an old native whom we knew well. For years he had been Sijefu's chief counsellor. Ndambe held up his hand. The line of women halted. Ndambe spoke. He declared that we white men were kings among kings and elephants among elephants. He also said that we were rinkhals snakes more poisonous and generally disgusting than any rinkhals snake in the country.

We knew, of course, that Ndambe was only paying us compliments in his ignorant Mtosa fashion. And so we naturally felt highly gratified. I can still remember the way Jurie Bekker nudged me in the ribs and said, "Did you hear that?"

When Ndambe went on, however, to say that we were filthier than the spittle of a green tree-toad, several burghers grew restive. They felt that there was perhaps such a thing as carrying these tribal courtesies a bit too far.

It was then that Veldkornet Joubert, slipping his finger inside the trigger guard of his gun, requested Ndambe to come to the point. By the expression on our veldkornet's face, you could see that he had had enough of compliments for one day.

They had come to offer peace, Ndambe told us then.

What the women carried on their heads were presents.

At a sign from Ndambe the column knelt in the mud of the turf-land. They brought lion and zebra skins and elephant tusks, and beads and brass bangles and, on a long grass mat, the whole haunch of a red Afrikaner ox, hide and hoof and all. And several pigs cut in half. And clay pots filled to the brim with white beer, and also – and this we prized most – witch-doctor medicines that protected you against goël spirits at night and the evil eye.

Ndambe gave another signal. A woman with a clay pot on her head rose up from the kneeling column and advanced towards us. We saw then that what she had in the pot was black earth. It was wet and almost like turf-soil. We couldn't understand what they wanted to bring us that for. As though we didn't have enough of it, right there where we were standing, and sticking to our veldskoens, and all. And yet Ndambe acted as though that was the most precious part of the peace offerings that his chief, Sijefu, had sent us.

It was when Ndambe spoke again that we saw how ignorant he and his chief and the whole Mtosa tribe were, really.

He took a handful of soil out of the pot and pressed it together between his fingers. Then he told us how honoured the Mtosa tribe was because we were waging war against them. In the past they had only had flat-faced Mshangaans with spiked knobkerries to fight against, he said, but now it was different. Our veldkornet took half a step forward, then, in case Ndambe was going to start flattering us again. So Ndambe said, simply, that the Mtosas would be glad if we came and made war against them later on, when the harvests had been gathered in. But in the meantime the tribe did not wish to continue fighting.

It was the time for sowing.

Ndambe let the soil run through his fingers, to show us how good it was. He also invited us to taste it. We declined.

We accepted the presents and peace was made. And I can still remember how Veldkornet Joubert shook his head and said, "Can you beat the Mtosas for ignorance?"

And I can still remember what Jurie Bekker said, also. That was when something made him examine the haunch of beef more closely, and he found his own brand mark on it.

It was not long afterwards that the war came against England.

By the end of the second year of the war the Boer forces were in a very bad way. But we would not make peace. Veldkornet Joubert was now promoted to kommandant. Combrinck fell in the battle before Dalmanutha. Jurie Bekker was still with us. And so was Fanie Louw. And it was strange how attached we had grown to Fanie Louw during the years of hardship that we went through together in the field. But up to the end we had to admit that, while we had got used to his jokes, and we knew there was no harm in them, we would have preferred it that he should stop making them.

He did stop, and for ever, in a skirmish near a blockhouse. We buried him in the shade of a thorn-tree. We got ready to fill in his grave, after which the kommandant would say a few words and we would bare our heads and sing a psalm. As you know, it was customary at a funeral for each mourner to take up a handful of earth and fling it in the grave.

When Kommandant Joubert stooped down and picked up his handful of earth, a strange thing happened. And I remembered that other war, against the Mtosas. And we knew – although we would not say it

– what was now that longing in the hearts of each of us. For Kommandant Joubert did not straightway drop the soil into Fanie Louw's grave. Instead, he kneaded the damp ground between his fingers. It was as though he had forgotten that it was funeral earth. He seemed to be thinking not of death, then, but of life.

We patterned after him, picking up handfuls of soil and pressing it together. We felt the deep loam in it, and saw how springy it was, and we let it trickle through our fingers. And we could remember only that it was the time for sowing.

I understood then how, in an earlier war, the Mtosas had felt, they who were also farmers.

The Red Coat

I have spoken before of some of the queer things that happen to your mind through fever (Oom Schalk Lourens said). In the past there was a good deal more fever in the Marico and Waterberg Districts than there is today. And you got it in a more severe form, too. Today you still get malaria in these parts, of course. But your temperature doesn't go so high anymore before the fever breaks. And you are not left as weak after an attack of malaria as you were in the old days. Nor do you often get illusions of the sort that afterwards came to trouble the mind of Andries Visagie.

They say that this improvement is due to civilisation.

Well, I suppose that must be right. For one thing, we now have a Government lorry from Zeerust every week with letters and newspapers and catalogues from Johannesburg shopkeepers. And only three years ago Jurie Bekker bought a wooden stand with a glass for measuring how much rain he gets on his farm. Jurie Bekker is very proud of his rain-gauge, too, and will accompany any white visitor to the back of his house to show him how well it works. "We have had no rain for the last three years," Jurie Bekker will explain, "and that is exactly what the rain-gauge records, also. Look, you can see for yourself – nil!"

Jurie Bekker also tried to explain the rain instrument to the kaffirs on his farm. But he gave it up. "A kaffir with a blanket on hasn't got the brain to understand a white man's inventions," Jurie Bekker said about it, afterwards. "When I showed my kaffirs what this rain-gauge was all about, they just stood in a long row and laughed."

Nevertheless, I must admit that, with all this civilisation we are getting here, the malaria fever has not of recent years been the scourge it was in the old days.

The story of Andries Visagie and his fever begins at the battle of Bronkhorstspruit. It was at the battle of Bronkhorstspruit that Andries Visagie had his life saved by Piet Niemand, according to all accounts. And yet it was also arising out of that incident that many people in this part of the Marico in later years came to the conclusion that Andries Visagie was somebody whose word you could not take seriously, because of the suffering that he had undergone.

You know, of course, that the Bronkhorstspruit battle was fought very long ago. In those days we still called the English 'redcoats.' For the English soldiers wore red jackets that we could see against the khaki colour of the tamboekie grass for almost as far as the bullets from our Martini-Henry rifles could carry. That shows you how uncivilised those times were.

I often heard Piet Niemand relate the story of how he found Andries Visagie lying unconscious in a donga on the battlefield, and of how he revived him with brandy that he had in his water-bottle.

Piet Niemand explained that, from the number of redcoats that were lined up at Bronkhorstspruit that morning, he could see it was going to be a serious engagement, and so he had thoughtfully emptied all the water out of his bottle and had replaced it with Magaliesberg peach brandy of the rawest kind he could get. Piet Niemand said that he was advancing against the English when he came across that donga. He was advancing very fast and was looking neither to right nor left of him, he said. And he would draw lines on any piece of paper that was handy to show you the direction he took.

I can still remember how annoyed we all were when a young schoolteacher, looking intently at that piece of paper, said that if that was the direction in which Piet Niemand was advancing, then it must have meant that the English had got right to behind the Boer lines, which was contrary to what he had read in the history books. Shortly afterwards Hannes Potgieter, who was chairman of our school committee, got that young school-teacher transferred.

As Hannes Potgieter said, that young school-teacher with his history-book ideas had never been in a battle and didn't know what real fighting was. In the confusion of a fight, with guns going off all round you, Hannes Potgieter declared, it was not unusual for a burgher to find himself advancing away from the enemy – and quite fast, too.

He was not ashamed to admit that a very similar thing had happened to him at one stage of the battle of Majuba Hill. He had run back a long way, because he had suddenly felt that he wanted to make sure that the kaffir agterryers were taking proper care of the horses. But he need have had no fears on that score, Hannes Potgieter added. Because when he reached the sheltered spot among the thorn-trees where the horses were tethered, he found that three kommandants and a veldkornet had arrived there before him, on the same errand. The veldkornet was so anxious to reassure himself that the horses were all right, that he was even trying to mount one of them.

When Hannes Potgieter said that, he winked. And we all laughed. For we knew that he had fought bravely at Majuba Hill. But he was also ready always to acknowledge that he had been very frightened at Majuba Hill. And because he had been in several wars, he did not like to hear the courage of Piet Niemand called in question. What Hannes Potgieter meant us to understand was that if, at the battle of Bronkhorstspruit, Piet Niemand did perhaps run at one stage, it was the sort of thing that could happen to any man; and for which any man could be forgiven, too.

And, in any case, Piet Niemand's story was interesting enough. He said that in the course of his advance he came across a donga, on the edge of which a thorn-bush was growing. The donga was about ten foot deep. He descended into the donga to light his pipe. He couldn't light his pipe out there on the open veld, because it was too windy, he said. When he reached the bottom of the donga, he also found that he had brought most of that thorn-bush along with him.

Then, in a bend of the donga, Piet Niemand saw what he thought was an English soldier, lying face downwards. He thought, at first, that the English soldier had come down there to light his pipe, also, and had decided to stay longer. He couldn't see too clearly, Piet Niemand said, because the smoke of the battle of Bronkhorstspruit had got into his eyes. Maybe the smoke from his pipe, too, I thought. That is, if what he was lighting up there in the donga was Piet Retief roll tobacco.

Why Piet Niemand thought that the man lying at the bend of the donga was an Englishman was because he was wearing a red coat. But in the next moment Piet Niemand realised that the man was not an Englishman. For the man's neck was not also red.

Immediately there flashed into Piet Niemand's mind the suspicion that the man was a Boer in English uniform – a Transvaal Boer fighting against his own people. If it had been an Englishman lying there, he would have called on him to surrender, Piet Niemand said, but a Boer traitor he was going to shoot without giving him a chance to get up.

He was in the act of raising his Martini-Henry to fire, when the truth came to him. And that was how he first met Andries Visagie and how he came to save his life. He saw that while Andries Visagie's coat was indeed red, it was not with dye, but with the blood from his wound. Piet Niemand said that he was so overcome at the thought of the sin he had been about to commit that when he unstrapped his water-bottle his knees trembled as much as did his fingers. But when Piet Niemand told this part of his story, Hannes Potgieter said that he need not make any excuses for himself, especially as no harm had come of it. If it had been a Boer traitor instead of Piet Niemand who had found himself in that same situation, Hannes Potgieter said, then the Boer traitor would have fired in any case, without bothering very much as to whether it was a Boer or an Englishman that he was shooting.

Piet Niemand knelt down beside Andries Visagie and turned him round and succeeded in pouring a quantity of brandy down his throat. Andries Visagie was not seriously wounded, but he had a high fever, from the sun and through loss of blood, and he spoke strange words.

That was the story that Piet Niemand had to tell.

Afterwards Andries Visagie made a good recovery in the mill at Bronkhorstspruit, that the kommandant had turned into a hospital. And they say it was very touching to observe Andries Visagie's gratitude when Piet Niemand came to visit him.

Andries Visagie lay on the floor, on a rough mattress filled with grass and dried mealie-leaves. Piet Niemand went and sat on the floor beside him. They conversed. By that time Andries Visagie had recovered sufficiently to remember that he had shot three redcoats for sure. He added, however, that as a result of the weakness caused by his wound, his mind was not very clear, at times. But when he got quite well and strong again, he would remember better. And then he would not be at all surprised if he remembered that he had also shot a general, he said.

Piet Niemand then related some of his own acts of bravery. And because they were both young men it gave them much pleasure to pass themselves off as heroes in each other's company.

Piet Niemand had already stood up to go when Andries Visagie reached his hand underneath the mattress and pulled out a watch with a heavy gold chain. The watch was shaped like an egg and on the case were pictures of angels, painted in enamel. Even without those angels, it would have been a very magnificent watch. But with those angels painted on the case, you would not care much if the watch did not go, even, and you still had to tell the time from the sun, holding your hand cupped over your eyes.

"I inherited this watch from my grandfather," Andries Visagie said. "He brought it with him on the Great Trek. You saved my life in the donga. You must take this watch as a keepsake."

Those who were present at this incident in the temporary hospital at Bronkhorstspruit said that Piet Niemand reached over to receive the gift. He almost had his hand on the watch, they say. And then he changed his mind and stood up straight.

"What I did was nothing," Piet Niemand said. "It was something anybody would have done. Anybody that was brave enough, I mean. But I want no reward for it. Maybe I'll some day buy myself a watch like that."

Andries Visagie kept his father's father's egg-shaped watch, after all. But in his having offered Piet Niemand his most treasured possession, and in Piet Niemand having declined to accept it, there was set the seal on the friendship of those two young men. This friendship was guarded, maybe, by the wings of the angels painted in enamel on the watch-case. Afterwards people were to say that it was a pity Andries Visagie should have turned so queer in the head. It must have been that he had suffered too much, these people said.

In gratitude for their services in the First Boer War, the Government of the Transvaal Republic made grants of farming land in the Waterberg District to those Boers on commando who had no ground of their own. The Government of the Transvaal Republic did not think it necessary to explain that the area in question was already occupied – by lions and malaria mosquitoes and hostile kaffirs. Nevertheless, many Boers knew the facts about that part of the Waterberg pretty well. So only a handful of burghers were prepared to accept Government farms. Most of the others felt that, seeing they had just come out of one war, there was not much point in going straight back into another.

All the same, a number of burghers did go and take up land in that area, and to everybody's surprise – not least to the surprise of the Government, I suppose – they fared reasonably well. And among those new settlers in the Waterberg were Piet Niemand and Andries Visagie. Their farms were not more than two days' journey apart. So you could almost say they were neighbours. They visited each other regularly.

The years went by, and then in a certain wet season Andries Visagie lay stricken with malaria. And in his delirium he said strange things. Fancying himself back again at Bronkhorstspruit, Andries Visagie said he could remember the long line of English generals he was shooting. He was shooting them full of medals, he said.

But there was another thing that Andries Visagie said he remembered then. And after he recovered from the malaria he still insisted that the circumstance he had recalled during his illness was the truth. He said that through that second bout of fever he was able to remember what had happened years before, in the donga, when he was also delirious.

And it was then that many of the farmers in the Waterberg began to say what a pity it was that Andries Visagie's illness should so far have affected his mind.

For Andries Visagie said that he could remember distinctly, now, that time when he was lying in the donga. And he would never, of course, know who shot him. But what he did remember was that when Piet Niemand was bending over him, holding a water-bottle in his hand, Piet Niemand was wearing a red coat.

The Question

Stefanus Malherbe had difficulty in getting access to the president, to put to him the question of which we were all anxious to learn the answer.

It was at Waterval Onder and President Kruger was making preparations to leave for Europe to enlist the help of foreign countries in the Transvaal's struggle against England. General Louis Botha had just been defeated at Dalmanutha. Accordingly, we who were the last of the Boer commandos in the field found ourselves hemmed in against the Portuguese border by the British forces, the few miles of railway-line from Nelspruit to Komatipoort being all that still remained to us of Transvaal soil. The Boer War had hardly begun, and it already looked like the end.

But when we had occasion to watch, from a considerable distance, a column of British dragoons advancing through a half-mile stretch of bush country, there were those of us who realised that the Boer War might, after all, not be over yet. It took the column two hours to get through that bush.

Although we who served under Veldkornet Stefanus Malherbe were appointed to the duty of guarding President Kruger during those last days, we had neither the opportunity nor the temerity to talk to him in that house at Waterval Onder. For one thing, there were those men with big stomachs and heavy gold watch-chains all crowding around the president with papers they wanted him to sign. Nevertheless, when the news came that the English had broken through at Dalmanutha, we overheard some of those men say, not raising their voices unduly, that something or other was no longer worth the paper it was written on. Next morning, when President Kruger again came on the front stoep of the house, alone this time, we were for the first time able to see him clearly, instead of through the thick screen of grey smoke being blown into his face from imported cigars.

"Well," Thys Haasbroek said, "I hope the president when he gets to Europe enlists the right kind of foreigners to come and fight for the Republic. It would be too bad if he came back with another crowd of uitlanders with big stomachs and watch-chains, waving papers for concessions."

I mention this remark made by one of the burghers then at Waterval Onder with the president to show you that there was not a uniform spirit of bitter-end loyalty animating the three thousand men who saw day by day the net of the enemy getting more tightly drawn around them. Indeed, speaking for myself, I must confess that the enthusiasm of those of our leaders who at intervals addressed us, exhorting us to courage, had but a restricted influence on my mind.

Especially when the orders came for the rolling stock to be dynamited.

For we had brought with us, in our retreat from Magersfontein, practically all the carriages and engines and trucks of the Transvaal and Orange Free State railways. At first we were much saddened by the necessity for destroying the property of our country. But afterwards something got into our blood which made it all seem like a good joke.

I know that our own little group that was under the leadership of Veldkornet Stefanus Malherbe really derived a considerable amount of enjoyment, towards the end, out of blowing railway engines and whole trains into the air. A couple of former shunters who were on commando with us would say things like, "There goes the Cape mail via Fourteen Streams." And we would fling ourselves into a ditch to escape the flying fragments of wood and steel. One of them also used to shout, "All seats for Bloemfontein," or "First stop Elandsfontein," after the fuse was lit and he would blow his whistle and wave a green flag. For several days it seemed that between Nelspruit and Hectorspruit you couldn't look up at any part of the sky without seeing wheels in it.

And during all this time we treated the whole affair as fun, and the former shunters had got to calling out, "There goes the 9.20 to De Aar against the signals" and, "There's a girl with fair hair travelling by herself in the end compartment." Being railwaymen, they couldn't think of anything else to say.

Because the war of the big commandos, and of men like Generals Joubert and Cronjé, was over, it seemed to us that all the fighting was just about done. We did not know that the Boer War of General de Wet and Ben Viljoen and General Muller was then only about to begin.

The next order that our veldkornet, Stefanus Malherbe, brought us from the kommandant was for the destruction of our stores and field guns and ammunition dumps as well. All we had to retain were our Mausers and horses, the order said. That did not give us much cause for hope. At the same time the first of General Louis Botha's burghers from the Dalmanutha fight began to arrive in our camp. They were worn out from their long retreat and many of them had acquired the singular habit of looking round over their shoulders very quickly, every so often, right in the middle of a conversation. Their presence did not help to inspire us with military ardour. One of these burghers was very upset at our having blown up all the trains. He had been born and bred in the gramadoelas and had been looking forward to his first journey by rail.

"I just wanted to feel how the thing rides," he said in disappointed tones, in between trying to wipe off stray patches of yellow lyddite stains he had got at Dalmanutha. "But even if there *was* still another train left, I suppose it would be too late, now."

"Yes, I am sure it would be too late," I said, also looking quickly over my shoulder. There was something infectious about this habit that Louis Botha's burghers had brought with them.

Actually, of course, it was not yet too late, for there was still a train, with the engine and carriages intact, waiting to take the president out of the Transvaal into Portuguese territory. There were also in the Boer ranks men whose loyalty to the Republic never wavered even in the darkest times. It had been a very long retreat from the northern Cape Province through the Orange Free State and the Transvaal to where we were now shut in near the Komati River. And it had all happened so quickly.

The Boer withdrawal, when once it got under way, had been very fast and very complete. I found it not a little disconcerting to think that on one day I had seen the president seated in a spider just outside Paardeberg drinking buttermilk and then on another day, only a few months later, I had seen him sitting on the front stoep of a house at Waterval Onder a thousand miles away, drinking brandy. Moreover, he was getting ready to move again.

"If it is only to Europe that he is going, then it is not too bad," said an old farmer with a long beard who was an ignorant man in many ways, but whose faith had not faltered throughout the retreat. "I would not have liked our beloved president to have to travel all that way back to the northern Cape where we started from. He hasn't the strength for so long a journey. I am glad that it is only to Russia that he is going."

Because he was not demoralised by defeat, as so many of us were, we who listened to this old farmer's words were touched by his simple loyalty. Indeed, the example set by men of his sort had a far greater influence on the course of the war during the difficult period ahead than the speeches that our leaders came round and made to us from time to time.

Certainly we did not feel that the veldkornet, Stefanus Malherbe, was a tower of strength. We did not dislike him nor did we distrust him. We only felt, after a peculiar fashion, that he was too much the same kind of man that we ourselves were. So we did not have overmuch respect for him.

I have said that we ordinary burghers did not have the temerity to approach the president and to talk to him as man to man of the matter that we wanted to know about. And so we hung back a little while Stefanus Malherbe, an officer on whom many weighty responsibilities reposed, put out his chest and strode toward the house to interview the president. "Put out your stomach," one of the burghers called out. He was of course thinking of those men who until lately had surrounded the president with their papers and watch-chains and cigars.

And then, when Stefanus Malherbe was moving in the direction of the voorkamer, where he knew the president to be, and when the rest of the members of our veldkornetskap had drawn ourselves together in a little knot that stood nervously waiting just off the stoep for the president's reply – I suppose it had to happen that just then a newly appointed general should have decided to treat us to a patriotic talk. Under other circumstances we would have been impressed, perhaps, but at that point in time, when we had already blown up our trains and stores and ammunition dumps, and had sunk the pieces that remained of the Staat's Artillerie in the Komati River – along with some papers we had captured in earlier battle – we were not an ideal audience.

We stood still, out of politeness, and listened. But all the time we were wondering if the veldkornet would perhaps be able to slip away at the end of the speech and manage to get in a few words with President Kruger after all. Anyway, I am sure that we took in very little of what the newly appointed general had to say.

In the end the general realised the position too. We gathered that he had known he was going to get the appointment that day, and that he had prepared a speech for the occasion, to deliver before the president and the State Council, but that he had been unable to have his say in the house because of the bustle attendant upon the president's impending departure. Consequently, the general delivered his set speech to us, the first group of burghers he encountered on his way out. After he had got us to sing Psalm 83 and had adjured each one of us to humble himself before the Lord, the general explained at great length that if we could perhaps not hope for victory, since victory might be beyond our capacity, we could still hope for a more worthy kind of defeat.

We made no response to his eloquence. We did not sweep our hats upward in a cheer. We did not call out, "Ou perd!" We were only concerned with the veldkornet's chances of getting in a word with the president before it was too late. The general understood, eventually, that our hearts were not in his address and so he concluded his speech rather abruptly. "Some defeats are greater than victories," he said, and he paused for a little while to survey us before adding, "but not this one, I don't think."

The meeting having ended suddenly like that, Veldkornet Stefanus Malherbe did, after all, manage to get into the voorkamer to speak to President Kruger alone. That much we knew. But when he came out of the house, the veldkornet was silent about his conversation with the president. He did not tell us what the president had said in answer to his question. And in the next advance of the English, which was made within that same week, and which took them right into Komatipoort, Veldkornet Stefanus Malherbe was killed. So he never told us what the president had said in answer to his question about the Kruger millions.

Peaches Ripening in the Sun

The way Ben Myburg lost his memory (Oom Schalk Lourens said) made a deep impression on all of us. We reasoned that that was the sort of thing that a sudden shock could do to you. There were those in our small section of General du Toit's commando who could recall similar stories of how people in a moment could forget everything about the past, just because of a single dreadful happening.

A shock like that can have the same effect on you even if you are prepared for it. Maybe it can be worse, even. And in this connection I often think of what it says in the Good Book, about that which you most feared having now at last caught up with you.

Our commando went as far as the border by train. And when the engine came to a stop on a piece of open veld, and it wasn't for water, this time, and the engine-driver and fireman didn't step down with a spanner and use bad language, then we understood that the train stopping there was the beginning of the Second Boer War.

We were wearing new clothes and we had new equipment, and the sun was shining on the barrels of our Mausers. Our new clothes had been requisitioned for us by our veldkornet at stores along the way. All the veldkornet had to do was to sign his name on a piece of paper for whatever his men purchased.

In most cases, after we had patronised a store in that manner, the shopkeeper would put up his shutters for the day. And three years would pass and the Boer War would be over before the shopkeeper would display any sort of inclination to take the shutters down again.

Maybe he should have put them up before we came.

Only one seksie of General du Toit's commando entered Natal looking considerably dilapidated. This seksie looked as though it was already the end of the Boer War, and not just the beginning. Afterwards we found out that their veldkornet had never learnt to write his name. We were glad that in the first big battle these men kept well to the rear, apparently conscious of how sinful they looked. For, to make matters worse, a regiment of Indian troops was fighting on that front, and we were not anxious that an Eastern race should see white men at such a disadvantage.

"You don't seem to remember me, Schalk," a young fellow came up and said to me. I admitted that I didn't recognise him, straight away, as Ben Myburg. He did look different in those smart light-green riding pants and that new hat with the ostrich feather stuck in it. You could see that he had patronised some mine concession store before the owner got his shutters down.

"But I would know you anywhere, Schalk," Ben Myburg went on. "Just from the quick way you hid that soap under your saddle a couple of minutes ago. I remembered where I had last seen something so quick. It was two years ago, at the Nagmaal in Nylstroom."

I told Ben Myburg that if it was that jar of brandy he meant, then he must realise that there had also been a good deal of misunderstanding about it. Moreover, it was not even a full jar, I said.

But I congratulated him on his powers of memory, which I said I was sure would yet stand the Republic in good stead.

And I was right. For afterwards, when the war of the big commandos was over, and we were in constant retreat, it would be Ben Myburg who, next day, would lead us back to the donga in which we had hidden some mealie-meal and a tin of cooking fat. And if the tin of cooking fat was empty, he would be able to tell us right away if it was kaffirs or baboons. A kaffir had a different way of eating cooking fat out of a tin from what a baboon had, Ben Myburg said.

Ben Myburg had been recently married to Mimi van Blerk, who came from Schweizer-Reneke, a district that was known as far as the Limpopo for its attractive girls. I remembered Mimi van Blerk well. She had full red lips and thick yellow hair. Ben Myburg always looked forward very eagerly to getting letters from his pretty young wife. He would also read out to us extracts from her letters, in which she encouraged us to drive the English into the blue grass – which was the name we gave to the sea in those days. For the English we had other names.

One of Mimi's letters was accompanied by a wooden candle-box filled with dried peaches. Ben Myburg was most proud to share out the dried fruit among our company, for he had several times spoken of the orchard of yellow cling peaches that he had laid out at the side of his house.

"We've already got dried peaches," Jurie Bekker said. Then he added, making free with our projected invasion of Natal: "In a few weeks' time we will be picking bananas."

It was in this spirit, as I have said, that we set out to meet the enemy. But nobody knew better than ourselves how much of this fine talk was to hide what we really felt. And I know, speaking for myself, that when we got the command "Opsaal", and we were crossing the border between the Transvaal and Natal, I was less happy at the thought that my horse was such a mettlesome animal. For it seemed to me that my horse was far more anxious to invade Natal than I was. I had to rein him in a good deal on the way to Spioenkop and Colenso. And I told myself that it was because I did not want him to go too fast downhill.

Eighteen months later saw the armed forces of the Republic in a worse case than I should imagine any army has ever been in, and that army still fighting. We were spread all over the country in small groups. We were in rags.

Many burghers had been taken prisoner. Others had yielded themselves up to British magistrates, holding not their rifles in their hands but their hats. There were a number of Boers, also, who had gone and joined the English.

For the Transvaal Republic it was near the end of a tale that you tell, sitting around the kitchen fire on a cold night. The story of the Transvaal Republic was at that place where you clear your throat before saying which of the two men the girl finally married. Or whether it was the cattle-smuggler or the Sunday school superintendent who stole the money. Or whether it was a real ghost or just her uncle with a sheet round him that Lettie van Zyl saw at the drift.

One night, when we were camped just outside Nietverdiend, and it was Ben Myburg's and my turn to go on guard, he told me that he knew that part well.

"You see that rant there, Schalk?" he asked. "Well, I have often stood on the other side of it, under the stars, just like now. You know, I've got a lot of peach trees on my farm. Well, I have stood there, under the ripening peaches, just after dark, with Mimi at my side. There is no smell like the smell of young peach trees in the evening, Schalk, when the fruit is ripening. I can almost imagine I am back there now. And it is just the time for it, too."

I tried to explain to Ben Myburg, in a roundabout way, that although everything might be exactly the same on this side of the rant, he would have to be prepared for certain changes on the other side, seeing that it was war.

Ben Myburg agreed that I was probably right. Nevertheless, he began to talk to me at length about his courtship days. He spoke of Mimi with her full red lips and her yellow hair.

"I can still remember the evening when Mimi promised that she would marry me, Schalk," Ben Myburg said. "It was in Zeerust. We were there for the Nagmaal. When I walked back to my tent on the kerkplein I was so happy that I just kicked the first three kaffirs I saw."

I could see that, talking to me while we stood on guard, Ben Myburg was living through that time all over again. I was glad, for their sakes, that no kaffirs came past at that moment. For Ben Myburg was again very happy.

I was pleased, too, for Ben Myburg's own sake, that he did at least have that hour of deep joy in which he could recall the past so vividly. For it was after that that his memory went.

By the following evening we had crossed the rant and had arrived at Ben Myburg's farm. We camped among the smoke-blackened walls of his former homestead, erecting a rough shelter with some sheets of corrugated iron that we could still use. And although he must have known only too well what to expect, yet what Ben Myburg saw there came as so much of a shock to his senses that from that moment all he could remember from the past vanished for ever.

It was pitiful to see the change that had come over him. If his farm had been laid to ruins, the devastation that had taken place in Ben Myburg's mind was no less dreadful.

Perhaps it was that, in truth, there was nothing more left in the past to remember.

We noticed, also, that in singular ways, certain fragments of the bygone would come into Ben Myburg's mind; and that he would almost – but not quite – succeed in fitting these pieces together.

We observed that almost immediately. For instance, we remained camped on his farm for several days. And one morning, when the fire for our mealie-pap was crackling under one of the few remaining fruit trees that had once been an orchard, Ben Myburg reached up and picked a peach that was, in advance of its season, ripe and yellow.

"It's funny," Ben Myburg said, "but I seem to remember, from long ago, reaching up and picking a yellow peach, just like this one. I don't quite remember where."

We did not tell him that he was picking one of his own peaches.

Some time later our seksie was captured in a night attack.

For us the Boer War was over. We were going to St. Helena. We were driven to Nylstroom, the nearest railhead, in a mule-wagon. It was a strange experience for us to be driving along the main road, in broad daylight, for all the world to see us. From years of war-time habit, our eyes still went to the horizon. A bitter thing about our captivity was that among our guards were men of our own people.

Outside Nylstroom we alighted from the mule-wagon and the English sergeant in charge of our escort got us to form fours by the roadside. It was queer – our having to learn to be soldiers at the end of a war instead of at the beginning.

Eventually we got into some sort of formation, the veldkornet, Jurie Bekker, Ben Myburg and I making up the first four. It was already evening. From a distance we could see the lights in the town. The way to the main street of Nylstroom led by the cemetery. Although it was dark, we could yet distinguish several rows of newly made mounds. We did not need to be told that they were concentration camp graves. We took off our battered hats and tramped on in a great silence.

Soon we were in the main street. We saw, then, what those lights were. There was a dance at the hotel. Paraffin lamps were hanging under the hotel's low, wide veranda. There was much laughter. We saw girls and English officers. In our unaccustomed fours we slouched past in the dark.

Several of the girls went inside, then. But a few of the womenfolk remained on the veranda, not looking in our direction. Among them I noticed particularly a girl leaning on an English officer's shoulder. She looked very pretty, with the light from a paraffin lamp shining on her full lips and yellow hair.

When we had turned the corner, and the darkness was wrapping us round again, I heard Ben Myburg speak.

"It's funny," I heard Ben Myburg say, "but I seem to remember, from long ago, a girl with yellow hair, just like that one. I don't quite remember where."

And this time, too, we did not tell him.

The Traitor's Wife

We did not like the sound of the wind that morning, as we cantered over a veld trail that we had made much use of, during the past year, when there were English forces in the neighbourhood.

The wind blew short wisps of yellow grass in quick flurries over the veld and the smoke from the fire in front of a row of kaffir huts hung low in the air. From that we knew that the third winter of the Boer War was at hand. Our small group of burghers dismounted at the edge of a clump of camel-thorns to rest our horses.

"It's going to be an early winter," Jan Vermeulen said, and from force of habit he put his hand up to his throat in order to close his jacket collar over in front. We all laughed, then. We realised that Jan Vermeulen had forgotten how he had come to leave his jacket behind when the English had surprised us at the spruit a few days before. And instead of a jacket, he was now wearing a mealie sack with holes cut in it for his head and arms. You could not just close over in front of your throat, airily, the lapels cut in a grain bag.

"Anyway, Jan, you're all right for clothes," Kobus Ferreira said, "but look at me."

Kobus Ferreira was wearing a missionary's frock-coat that he had found outside Kronendal, where it had been hung on a clothes-line to air.

"This frock-coat is cut so tight across my middle and shoulders that I have to sit very stiff and awkward in my saddle, just like the missionary sits on a chair when he is visiting at a farmhouse," Kobus Ferreira added. "Several times my horse has taken me for an Englishman, in consequence of the way I sit. I am only afraid that when a bugle blows my horse will carry me over the rant into the English camp."

At Kobus Ferreira's remark the early winter wind seemed to take on a keener edge.

For our thoughts went immediately to Leendert Roux, who had been with us on commando a long while and who had been spoken of as a likely man to be veldkornet – and who had gone scouting, one night, and did not come back with a report.

There were, of course, other Boers who had also joined the English. But there was not one of them that we had respected as much as we had done Leendert Roux.

Shortly afterwards we were on the move again.

In the late afternoon we emerged through the Crocodile Poort that brought us in sight of Leendert Roux's farmhouse. Next to the dam was a patch of mealies that Leendert Roux's wife had got the kaffirs to cultivate.

"Anyway, we'll camp on Leendert Roux's farm and eat roast mealies tonight," our veldkornet, Apie Theron, observed.

"Let us first rather burn his house down," Kobus Ferreira said. And in a strange way it seemed as though his violent language was not out of place in a missionary's frock-coat. "I would like to roast mealies in the thatch of Leendert Roux's house."

Many of us were in agreement with Kobus.

But our veldkornet, Apie Theron, counselled us against that form of vengeance.

"Leendert Roux's having his wife and farmstead here will yet lead to his undoing," the veldkornet said. "One day he will risk coming out here on a visit, when he hasn't got Kitchener's whole army at his back. That will be when we will settle our reckoning with him."

We did not guess that that day would be soon.

The road we were following led past Leendert Roux's homestead. The noise of our horses' hooves brought Leendert Roux's wife, Serfina, to the door. She stood in the open doorway and watched us riding by. Serfina was pretty, taller than most women, and slender, and there was no expression in her eyes that you could read, and her face was very white.

It was strange, I thought, as we rode past the homestead, that the sight of Serfina Roux did not fill us with bitterness.

Afterwards, when we had dismounted in the mealie-lands, Jan Vermeulen made a remark at which we laughed.

"For me it was the worst moment in the Boer War," Jan Vermeulen said. "Having to ride past a pretty girl, and me wearing just a sack. I was glad there was Kobus Ferreira's frock-coat for me to hide behind."

Jurie Bekker said there was something about Serfina Roux that reminded him of the Transvaal. He did not know how it was, but he repeated that, with the wind of early winter fluttering her skirts about her ankles, that was how it seemed to him.

Then Kobus Ferreira said that he had wanted to shout out something to her when we rode past the door, to let Serfina know how we, who were fighting in the last ditch – and in unsuitable clothing – felt about the wife of a traitor. "But she stood there so still," Kobus Ferreira said, "that I just couldn't say anything. I felt I would like to visit her, even."

That remark of Kobus Ferreira's fitted in with his frock-coat, also. It would not be the first time a man in ecclesiastical dress called on a woman while her husband was away.

Then, once again, a remark of Jan Vermeulen's made us realise that there was a war on. Jan Vermeulen had taken the mealie sack off his body and had threaded a length of baling-wire above the places where the holes were. He was now restoring the grain bag to the use it had been meant for, and I suppose that, in consequence, his views generally also got sensible.

"Just because Serfina Roux is pretty," Jan Vermeulen said, flinging mealie heads into the sack, "let us not forget who and what she is. Perhaps it is not safe for us to camp tonight on this farm. She is sure to be in touch with the English. She may tell them where we are. Especially now that we have taken her mealies."

But our veldkornet said that it wasn't important if the English knew where we were. Indeed, any kaffir in the neighbourhood could go and report our position to them. But what did matter was that we should know where the English were. And he reminded us that in two years he had never made a serious mistake that way.

"What about the affair at the spruit, though?" Jan Vermeulen asked him. "And my pipe and tinder-box were in the jacket, too."

By sunset the wind had gone down. But there was a chill in the air. We had pitched our camp in the tamboekie grass on the far side of Leendert Roux's farm. And I was glad, lying in my blankets, to think that it was the turn of the veldkornet and Jurie Bekker to stand guard.

Far away a jackal howled. Then there was silence again. A little later the stillness was disturbed by sterner sounds of the veld at night. And those sounds did not come from very far away, either. They were sounds Jurie Bekker made – first, when he fell over a beacon, and then when he gave his opinion of Leendert Roux for setting up a beacon in the middle of a stretch of dubbeltjie thorns. The blankets felt very snug, pulled over my shoulders, when I reflected on those thorns.

And because I was young, there came into my thoughts, at Jurie Bekker's mention of Leendert Roux, the picture of Serfina as she had stood in front of her door.

The dream I had of Serfina Roux was that she came to me, tall and graceful, beside a white beacon on her husband's farm. It was that haunting kind of dream, in which you half know all the time that you are dreaming. And she was very beautiful in my dream. And it was as though her hair was hanging half out of my dream and reaching down into the wind when she came closer to me. And I knew what she wanted to tell me. But I did not wish to hear it. I knew that if Serfina spoke that thing I would wake up from my dream. And in that moment, like it always happens in a dream, Serfina did speak.

"Opskud, kêrels!" I heard.

But it was not Serfina who gave that command. It was Apie Theron, the veldkornet. He came running into the camp with his rifle at the trail. And Serfina was gone. In a few minutes we had saddled our horses and were ready to gallop away. Many times during the past couple of years our scouts had roused us thus when an English column was approaching.

We were already in the saddle when Apie Theron let us know what was toward. He had received information, he said, that Leendert Roux had that very night ventured back to his homestead. If we hurried we might trap him in his own house. The veldkornet warned us to take no chances, reminding us that when Leendert Roux had still stood on our side he had been a fearless and resourceful fighter.

So we rode back during the night along the same way we had come in the afternoon. We tethered our horses in a clump of trees near the mealie-land and started to surround the farmhouse. When we saw a figure running for the stable at the side of the house, we realised that Leendert Roux had been almost too quick for us.

In the cold, thin wind that springs up just before the dawn we surprised Leendert Roux at the door of his stable. But when he made no resistance it was almost as though it was Leendert Roux who had taken us by surprise. Leendert Roux's calm acceptance of his fate made it seem almost as though he had never turned traitor, but that he was laying down his life for the Transvaal.

In answer to the veldkornet's question, Leendert Roux said that he would be glad if Kobus Ferreira – he having noticed that Kobus was wearing the frock-coat of a man of religion – would read Psalm 110 over his grave. He also said that he did not want his eyes bandaged. And he asked to be allowed to say goodbye to his wife.

Serfina was sent for. At the side of the stable, in the wind of early morning, Leendert and Serfina Roux, husband and wife, bade each other farewell.

Serfina looked even more shadowy than she had done in my dream when she set off back to the homestead along the footpath through the thorns. The sun was just beginning to rise. And I understood how right Jurie Bekker had been when he said that she was just like the Transvaal, with the dawn wind fluttering her skirts about her ankles as it rippled the grass. And I remembered that it was the Boer women that kept on when their menfolk recoiled before the steepness of the Drakensberge and spoke of turning back.

I also thought of how strange it was that Serfina should have come walking over to our camp, in the middle of the night, just as she had done in my dream. But where my dream was different was that she had reported not to me but to our veldkornet where Leendert Roux was.

Notes on the Text

Six of the stories gathered here ("Treasure Trove", "Unto Dust", "The Homecoming", "Susannah and the Play-actor," "Oom Piet's Party" and "Funeral Earth") were published only once in Bosman's lifetime, with no manuscript or typescript versions of these surviving. These published versions were therefore used as copy-texts here. A somewhat contrasting case is "The Red Coat", which was not published in English in Bosman's lifetime and exists only in the form of a single typescript (used here).

The remaining stories have more complicated textual histories: often two or more typescripts exist and the stories were themselves sometimes published more than once by Bosman. What follows is a description of each story's textual history and an explanation of the choices I have made in each case.

"Romaunt of the Smuggler's Daughter": one typescript and one published version. The published version used the title "The Romance of the Smuggler's Daughter", but is otherwise very close to the typescript. I have followed the typescript because the published version contains numerous errors and appears unreliable. I have also (like Lionel Abrahams and others) reverted to the more colourful "Romaunt" first used in the title by Bosman.

"The Picture of Gysbert Jonker": one typescript and one published version. The published version has been followed because the typescript is clearly an earlier version.

"The Ferreira Millions": two typescripts and one published version. The second typescript and the published version are very similar. I have followed the published version because it appeared in *The Forum* in Bosman's lifetime and is more reliable.

"Bush Telegraph": one typescript version, which I have used here. Fragments of typescripts of a closely related story ("The Kaffir Drum") exist, and these Abrahams used, together with the "Bush Telegraph" typescript and his own translation of Bosman's "Die Kaffertamboer", to piece together a complete story. However, the result, "The Kafir Drum", which appears in Abrahams's *Unto Dust*, is largely a work of translation by Abrahams (as he acknowledges in his editor's note), and I have preferred to revert to the earlier Bosman typescript "Bush

Telegraph." The respective merits of the two stories may be debated, but in the end what we have here is a complete Bosman story that required very little editorial intervention on my part.

"Sold Down the River": one manuscript, two typescripts and one published version. The second of these typescripts is identical to the version published in *The South African Jewish Times* (Sept., 1949), which I have used here.

"Tryst by the Vaal": two typescript versions. The first of these is untitled and is much longer than the other, titled "Tryst by the Vaal." The first typescript was translated into Afrikaans by Bosman and appeared as "Ontmoetingplek aan die Vaal" in *On Parade* in May, 1949. (Like several other stories in this collection, it was republished recently in its Afrikaans version in *Verborge Skatte*, edited by Leon de Kock for the Anniversary Edition in 2001 – as "Ontmoetingsplek aan die Vaal.") "Tryst by the Vaal" was chosen here because it is clearly a later, tighter version.

"The Lover Who Came Back": one manuscript, one typescript and two published versions. The manuscript was clearly a first draft and was followed by the typescript, which bears the title "The Stile." (Abrahams used this typescript as his copy-text and adopted the title "The Stile" when he printed the story in his *Unto Dust*.) The story appeared as "The Lover Who Came Back" in both *The Star* (July, 1949) and *The Sunday Tribune* (Sept., 1949). I have used the second of these published versions, as it was tightened up in small but cumulatively significant ways. I have also settled for the title that Bosman chose to use in both published versions.

"The Selon's Rose": one manuscript and two typescripts. (The story was published in Afrikaans in *On Parade* in Sept., 1949 as "Ou Liedjies en Ou Stories", but did not appear in English in Bosman's lifetime.) The second typescript version has been used here, and the English "The Selon's Rose" rather than the Afrikaans-derived "The Selons-rose" adopted as the title.

"When the Heart is Eager": one typescript and one published version. These versions are very similar, but I have followed the published one because there are small improvements in it. The typescript was originally titled "When the Heart is Eager"; this was crossed out by Bosman and "Past Roses and Brown Water" added by hand. Abrahams changed this to "Pink Roses and Brown Water." Because of this confusion, I have reverted to the title used by Bosman when he published the story.

"The Brothers": one manuscript, three typescripts and one published version. While Abrahams used the slightly longer, penultimate typescript version, I have found the version published in *The Forum* tighter, suggesting that Bosman re-edited the story before submitting it for publication.

"The Missionary": one fragment of a manuscript, one complete typescript, some additional manuscript notes marked for inclusion in the typescript and one published version. Abrahams reconstructed a complete version out of the manuscripts and typescript. I have followed the published version, as it was probably Bosman's final, preferred version.

"The Question": two typescripts and one published version. I have used the second of the typescript versions, as the version published posthumously in *Personality* appeared unreliable.

"Peaches Ripening in the Sun": one typescript and one published version. These versions are very different. The published one is a lot more concise, and is clearly the one Bosman preferred; I have therefore followed it here.

"The Traitor's Wife": three typescripts and one published version. The last typescript and the published version are very similar. I have used the published version as a basic copy-text, but incorporated the section breaks reflected in the last typescript, as the layout of the published version was erratic.

Because of what it reveals of Bosman's working methods, it is worth dwelling at length on the revisions Bosman made to a late piece of his such as "The Traitor's Wife", for example. Other stories from this volume – "Tryst by the Vaal" and "Peaches Ripening in the Sun" are two further examples – were revised in a very similar fashion, and so the discussion that follows can be taken to apply to many of Bosman's later stories.

The three typescripts relating to "The Traitor's Wife" take the form of a fourteen (half-)page version, a seven-page one and a six-page one which is closest to the version published in *Spotlight*. I will confine my attention to the seven-page typescript version and compare aspects of it with the version published in *Spotlight*. The two versions are not appreciably different as regards the main thrust of the story: the key details are the same and the same poignant ending is attempted. The crucial differences between the two are in their *style*: in essence, the typescript version works by explanation and interpretation, whereas the published version works by subtle implication and inference.

Many of the changes were made simply to tighten up the story. (An invariable characteristic of Bosman's revisions was his tendency to edit – sometimes quite ruthlessly – in order to achieve a sparse, pared-down style and a tantalisingly elliptical quality.) For example, when the men arrive for the first time at Leendert Roux's farm, the following passage, which occurs in the typescript version, was subsequently deleted: "It was the only farmhouse still standing in that area. The English would naturally spare the homestead of a man who was fighting on their side." The remark is unnecessary: it is obvious that men fighting a protracted, losing war would be bitter about the treachery of a former comrade.

There are also some telling additions. Two satirical comments about the untrustworthiness of men of the cloth were added to the typescript by hand. The first instance occurs when the men speak about setting up camp on Leendert Roux's farm and Kobus Ferreira caustically remarks: "'Let us first rather burn his house down.'" This was originally followed in the typescript version by: ". . . his violent language seeming to contrast rather unhappily with his ecclesiastical frock-coat." No doubt Bosman later spotted the satirical potential in the situation and changed the passage to read: "And in a strange way it seemed as though his violent language was not out of place in a missionary's frock-coat."

The other instance is when Kobus Ferreira remarks that he would have liked to shout out something to Serfina about how the men felt about the wife of a traitor, but that he could not bring himself to do so: "'I just couldn't say anything. I felt I would like to visit her, even.'" In the final version Bosman added Schalk Lourens's ironic comment: "It would not be the first time a man in ecclesiastical dress called on a woman while her husband was away."

The last movement of the story was extensively cut. The typescript contains long passages describing the capture of Roux and his response to his predicament. I wish to quote these in their entirety because they give a clear sense of how Bosman transformed the typescript version into the much tighter, more effective published version. The underlined parts are those later deleted by Bosman; the phrases and sentences in square brackets are those he added by hand to link the passages left after his drastic pruning:

In the cold, thin wind that springs up just before the dawn we surprised Leendert Roux at the door of his stable. But when he made no resistance it was almost as though it was Leendert Roux who had taken us by surprise.

We escorted him to behind the stable in order to get out of the wind. And all the while the man who had once been a member of our commando said it was right that we were going to shoot him. Leendert Roux's calm acceptance of his fate unnerved us. If he had struggled, as we had expected him to do, or if we had to burn his house down on top of him to get him out – as happened with a renegade burgher in the Rustenburg district – then our task would not have been hard.

But now it all seemed different. Because Leendert Roux kept on insisting that it was right that he should die for his sin, [made] it seemed in a strange way almost as though he had never turned traitor, but that he was laying down his life for the Transvaal. And in a way, I suppose, he was. It is difficult to explain these feelings. But that was how we did indeed feel that morning.

The veldkornet asked if he had a last request to make. [In answer to the veldkornet's question,] Leendert Roux said that he would be glad if Kobus Ferreira – he having noticed that Kobus was wearing the frock-coat of a man of religion – would read Psalm 110 over his grave. He also said that he did not want his eyes bandaged. And he asked to be allowed to see his wife for the last time [say goodbye to his wife].

Serfina was sent for. Their final leave-taking of each other, Leendert and Serfina Roux, husband and wife, behind the stable, in the wind of the early morning, was very touching. For a while they stood in each other's arms without speaking. Then Leendert Roux spoke. "It is right, Serfina," he said, "that I should die for my guilt." We could see Serfina's hesitation. Then she answered, in a firm voice, "Yes, my husband, it is right."

After his wife had kissed him farewell, Leendert said again, "You know, Serfina, I am glad that it has ended this way." Serfina did not answer. Her lips parted slightly, and palely, just as they had parted in my dream, and she looked as beautiful, then, as she had looked in my dream. Only, she looked even more shadowy, somehow, there, at the back of the stable, than any vision that comes to one in the night.

With her lips still slightly apart, Serfina turned from her husband and gazed for a moment into the face of the nearest burgher. If she had asked us to spare her husband's life then, who knows but that we might not have been able to refuse her. Apie Theron, for one, would have found it very difficult. Determined and fearless though he was in all things, our veldkornet yet was in certain ways the most soft-hearted of us all.

Serfina's hesitation lasted only for that single instant. But it was long enough for Leendert Roux to realise why his wife was faltering. "No, Serfina," he called out to her. It is right that this should be." [At the side of the stable, in the wind of early morning, Leendert and Serfina Roux, husband and wife, bade each other farewell.]

Serfina [looked even more shadowy than she had done in my dream when she] set off [back to the homestead] along the footpath through the thorns that led back to the house. The sun was just beginning to rise. And I understood how right Jurie Bekker had been when he said that she was just like the Transvaal, with the dawn wind fluttering her skirts about her ankles as it rippled the grass. And I thought of [remembered that it was] the Boer women that kept on when their menfolk recoiled before the steepness of the Drakensberge and spoke of turning back.

And I understood how great was Serfina's love for her husband, and her abiding faith in him, that she should have been able to walk [I also thought of how strange it was that Serfina should have come walking] over to our camp, in the middle of the night, just as she had done in my dream. But where my dream was different was that she had reported not to me but to our veldkornet where Leendert Roux was.

The first deleted parts relate to Roux's reaction to his capture and his repeated assertion that what was about to befall him was just and right. Oom Schalk then observes that this makes the men's task all the more difficult. Bosman's pruning here allows a leaner passage to emerge in which Roux is shown to be courageous and stoical. His calm resignation acquires a mysterious aura which is not present in the over-written, over-explanatory typescript version.

The middle sections describe the interaction between man and wife. But we don't *need* to be told how poignant the situation is. And Leendert's assertion once again about the fitness of his fate begins to wear thin by this point: indeed, the reader starts to wonder whether he is being sincere or is desperately trying to convince himself. His stoical, mysterious aura has all but been dispelled. And Serfina's affirmation of his sentiment is also unnecessary: the reader will find out very shortly that it was she who betrayed him and that she therefore quite obviously believes that he deserves his fate. The extended descriptions of Serfina are engaging, but they do tend to verge on the mawkish, and her beauty and serene detachment are far more effectively conveyed in the edited version. They also carry a suggestion of lasciviousness on Oom Schalk's part – something that would have sat ill with the stark poignancy of the closing passages.

The final deleted passages relate to Serfina's hesitation. These are more effective and perhaps have a stronger claim to retention, but they also would have served to remove some of *her* mystery and aura. It is her resoluteness, in the face of her undeniable love for her husband (which, again, we don't need to hear about in the last paragraph – "And I understood how great was Serfina's love for her husband, and her abiding faith in him. . . "), that gives her the iconic status adumbrated by Oom Schalk's evocation of the Boer women who "kept on when their menfolk recoiled before the steepness of the Drakensberge and spoke of turning back."

In sum, what the severely pruned published version achieves is a kind of austere beauty entirely commensurate with the tragic poignancy of the story. This quality would have been compromised by the earlier passages had they been retained. Like Pauline Smith's finest stories (and Bosman, of course, was a great admirer of his skilful part-contemporary), "The Traitor's Wife" leaves the reader with a desire to read more into the sparse details left on the page.

For example, it occurs to the reader that Serfina in all likelihood spent some of the very night on which she betrayed her husband making love to him. He probably returned soon after nightfall, while she did not alert the commando until close to dawn. Perhaps he himself suspected that she would do this, and resigned himself to his fate when he realised that his own wife had indeed betrayed him – and that, moreover, she was *right* to do so.

The pared-down version, then, requires much more active interpretation on the part of the reader. Through this activity the unspoken aspects of the story become tacitly understood. The reader is left in little doubt that Serfina *did* love her husband, but felt torn by two powerful and irreconcilable allegiances: to her husband, and to her despoiled and forlorn country. Therein lies the power and tragedy of the story.

For his part, Leendert Roux remains in the reader's mind as a compelling, equally tragic figure. We are left to speculate as to why a once brave, resolute fighter goes over to the other side. And his quiet resignation at the end partly restores his former stature, confirming perhaps that he (like all of us) is both brave and cowardly, noble and self-serving.

The stories are printed here largely in the sequence in which they were first published. "The Red Coat" and "The Question", which were unpublished in Bosman's lifetime and which cannot therefore be dated (Bosman never dated his manuscripts), have been inserted at appropriate points into the cluster of Boer War stories that concludes this collection. A minor liberty was taken in order to preserve this cluster: "The Missionary" was published slightly after "Funeral Earth" but has been placed immediately before it here. Similarly, "The Ferreira Millions" and "Sold Down the River" have been moved up to just after "Treasure Trove" and "Susannah and the Play-actor", respectively, so that the two pairs of stories can be read as variations on a theme. The two previously unpublished stories ("Bush Telegraph" and "Tryst by the Vaal") have been situated around the dates on which their Afrikaans near-equivalents appeared.

Versions of stories used as copy-texts here (an asterisk indicates a previously unpublished story):

1. "Romaunt of the Smuggler's Daughter." Undated typescript, Harry Ransom Humanities Research Center (HRHRC). First published as "The Romance of the Smuggler's Daughter" in *The Sunday Tribune* 19 Sept 1948: 22, 25.
2. "The Picture of Gysbert Jonker." *On Parade* 22 Oct 1948: 4–5.
3. "Treasure Trove." *Trek* 12.10 (Oct 1948): 18–19.
4. "The Ferreira Millions." *The Forum* 13.1 (1 Apr 1950): 24–25.
5. "Unto Dust." *Trek* 13.2 (Feb 1949): 18–19.
6. *"Bush Telegraph." Undated typescript, HRHRC.
7. "The Homecoming." *On Parade* 16 Mar 1949: 10.
8. "Susannah and the Play-actor." *On Parade* 14 Apr 1949: 10.
9. "Sold Down the River." *The South African Jewish Times* Sept 1949: 25.
10. *"Tryst by the Vaal." Undated typescript, HRHRC.
11. "The Lover Who Came Back." *The Sunday Tribune* 18 Sept 1949: 20. First published in *The Star* 23 July 1949: 7.

12. "The Selon's Rose." Undated typescript, HRHRC. First published in *Unto Dust* (1963): 133–39.
13. "When the Heart is Eager." *The Forum* 12.26 (1 Oct 1949): 20–21.
14. "The Brothers." *The Forum* 12.44 (4 Feb 1950): 24–25.
15. "Oom Piet's Party." *Sunday Express Supplement* 28 May 1950: 14–15.
16. "The Missionary." *Spotlight* Jan 1951: 14–15.
17. "Funeral Earth." *Vista*. Johannesburg: Council of Cultural Societies, University of the Witwatersrand, 1950: 62–65.
18. "The Red Coat." Undated typescript, HRHRC. First published in *Makapan's Caves and Other Stories* (1987): 30–36.
19. "The Question." Undated typescript, HRHRC. First published in *Personality* 14 Aug 1969: 139–41.
20. "Peaches Ripening in the Sun." *On Parade* 27 Feb 1951: 12–13.
21. "The Traitor's Wife." *Spotlight* Feb 1951: 6–7, 57.

My grateful thanks to Pat Fox of the Harry Ransom Humanities Research Center at the University of Texas at Austin and to Mpho Mathebula and Judith Benyon of the National Library of South Africa (Pretoria Branch) for invaluable help in tracing material at various stages of this project.